---------------★---------------

I almost didn't go on. Every nerve ending I owned was shouting *Leave, run, get out of here,* but I had to go on. One foot in front of the other, I slowly approached the door, pulled it open, and looked in. The fluorescent lights gave me a clear view of what lay on the black-and-white kitchen floor. I stopped, hand over my mouth, and for a moment forgot to breathe. Dottie. Like a rag doll a child had dropped, she lay on the floor, eyes staring, the front of her yellow sweatshirt stained bright red.

Oh my God, I thought wildly. *No, this can't be happening. Not again.*

I rushed in, called her name, and knelt beside her, but I knew there was no hope. Her open eyes were blank, and no breath disturbed the blood that still dripped slowly from her sweatshirt. I waited for the waves of nausea to subside, then looked around for a phone. There was one on the wall, and with a trembling hand, I dialed 911.

I kept trying not to look at her. Sweet, anxious Dottie. What had she wanted to tell me? Who had killed her? Why? She knew something... she must have. But what?

DYING
FOR A
CHANGE

KATHLEEN DELANEY

TORONTO • NEW YORK • LONDON
AMSTERDAM • PARIS • SYDNEY • HAMBURG
STOCKHOLM • ATHENS • TOKYO • MILAN
MADRID • WARSAW • BUDAPEST • AUCKLAND

Recycling programs
for this product may
not exist in your area.

DYING FOR A CHANGE

A Worldwide Mystery/September 2012

First published by PublishAmerica.com

ISBN-13: 978-0-373-63644-0

Copyright © 2002 by Kathleen Delaney

Printed in U.S.A.

Acknowledgments

This book is dedicated to my mother, Winifred Delaney. Her suggestions and support in this, as in all things in my life, have been invaluable. Thanks, Mom.

ONE

THE KEY WENT in but refused to work. I could feel tumblers move, but the door stubbornly stayed locked. I felt something else. Rain. It had been teasing all day and chose now, as I stood on the unprotected front porch, to let go. Water descended on my hair, slid under my collar and down the small of my back.

"Damn," I said, and viciously poked the doorbell, more from frustration than hope. The house was unoccupied. The first clients in my one-week real estate career were due momentarily, and I couldn't get in.

"Why are you doing this to me?" I shouted at the closed door. I grabbed the knob and rattled it.

It opened.

One leap and I was in the entryway, shuddering, shivering and shaking like a dog. Of course! The door hadn't been locked in the first place. I found a rumpled tissue in my jacket pocket, used it to mop my hair and looked around. The blackening sky outside dimmed the entry and made shadows of the doorways. Lights. I needed lights.

Was there electricity? The doorbell had chimed. A good sign. I found a switch and flicked it. Immediately the overhead chandelier bathed the tile floor with light and chased away the darkness that had hidden the living room.

That's better, I thought, letting hope return. Maybe there were other lights that worked. Maybe I'd actually be able to show this large, new house, and maybe the couple that called into the office only an hour ago would brave the rain and show up. If they didn't, I'd never find them again. Unfortunately, in the excitement of making my first appointment, I'd forgotten to get their name and phone number. Tom Chambers, one of the agents training me at Harper's Land Sales, had all but rolled on the floor with laughter. His wife, Nicole, had been more tactful.

"It's all right, Ellen," she'd said. "You can get all that when you meet with them. Here." She handed me a file filled with papers. "In case they want to make an offer. You do know how to fill these out?"

"Of course," I'd lied.

Nicole looked doubtful, but I'd taken the folder and fled.

I stood in the living room window, clutching my folder tightly, and looked down the street. Would they want to make an offer? Both real estate school and Sharon Harper, owner of the office where I now worked, had shown me how to fill out an offer form, but everything I'd learned seemed to have disappeared. Could I put them off until tomorrow? Meet them in the office, with Sharon safely beside me? But maybe they wouldn't like this house, and would want to see others. I tried to think of all the houses I'd seen this past week. I couldn't remember one of them. *I'm panicking. Have to relax. It's only because it's the first time, it'll get easier after this.* I took a deep breath, made my fingers quit crunching the folder, and looked at my watch.

I was to meet them at four. It was only one minute past. Fourteen minutes to go before I could reasonably conclude they weren't going to show, another five before I could leave, relief and dejection equally mixed.

The unrelenting rain rapidly turned the unplanted front yard into a muddy lake. It turned the dust on the empty truck parked by the side of the house into brown streaks.... Truck? Where had that come from? Where was the driver? I thought about the unlocked front door and froze. Maybe I wasn't alone.

I held my breath and listened. Stepping away from the window, I heard a creak, and froze again. It took a second to realize it was my foot on the uncarpeted floorboards. Fear propelled me into the living room—there, a light switch. Ah—light.

For a second I stood, hoping to hear the sound of a car. Nothing but the steady beat of rain. Another glance at my watch, only three minutes past four. All right. I'd have to wait, but not in the dark. Flicking each switch, I felt more confident as I blazed the downstairs rooms with light.

At the base of the stairs, I stopped.

Real estate school had stressed, among other things, that female agents should never, ever, meet clients any place but in the office. Here I was, meeting someone whose name I didn't know, waiting in an empty house where a strange truck stood outside the front door, its driver nowhere to be seen. Was the driver waiting for me? Lurking somewhere, ready to pounce...

"Ellen McKenzie," I told myself, "you've lost it. You don't live in the city anymore. This is little old Santa Louisa. Nothing has ever happened here, and never will!"

Right. Sure. I'd been gone from Santa Louisa for over twenty years, and things had changed. Not that my tiny hometown was experiencing a crime wave. However... Maybe I'd just check the street for my clients.

The downpour had eased into gentle rain, making it easy to see no car was in sight. This time my watch said ten after four, and I was out of excuses. Turning back to the staircase, I took a deep breath and headed up.

Work on the house hadn't quite finished. The toilet sat in the hallway, waiting to be installed in the tile-floored bathroom. A bucket of paint sat beside some leftover pieces of crown molding leaning against the wall in the master bedroom. A scattering of bricks lay next to the fireplace. It looked as though someone had pushed over the pile. Probably not. Just leftovers, carelessly stacked. I admired the federal mantel, tried to see the street from the French doors, flooded the master bath with a soft florescent glow and spent a moment envying some lucky person the luxurious bathtub. Ah, the walk-in closet. Everyone in the office had talked about how spacious it was, how convenient, how…occupied. A man lay on what should have been an empty closet floor. A bloody, bashed, and very dead man.

TWO

NOTHING MOVED AS I stared at the body. My heart didn't beat, my blood didn't flow, and my lungs didn't pump air.

Then everything worked at once, and I screamed. The sound echoed around the closet and bounced out at me, vibrating in my head. Legs and feet still held me up, and I propelled myself out of the bedroom, into the hallway and down the stairs.

"Omph," I exclaimed. I'd run into a large, rather soft chest, covered by a damp warm-up jacket.

"Hey," the man said.

He stood on the step below me, his round face level with mine.

"Hey," he repeated, and reached for my arm. "What's…"

"Oh, no," I screamed in his face, then pushed hard at him and tried to retreat back up the stairs. A dead body in a closet, the murderer on the stairs, and me in the middle. Real estate was turning out to be harder than I expected.

The man clutched my arm and grabbed the banister to steady himself as I struggled to get away.

"What's the matter? What's going on here? Hey, quit screaming," he shouted in my ear.

I stopped and took a better look at this man who had me by the arm. Middle-aged, overweight, round blue eyes that peered from under the brim of a shapeless rain hat, he seemed more alarmed than menacing.

"What is it, Harvey? What's the matter?"

The timid voice came from the bottom of the stairs. It belonged to a small woman wrapped in a large brown raincoat, wearing another dripping rain hat.

"I don't know, Bernice. That's what I'm trying to find out. Now!" He gave my arm, which he still held, a little shake. "What's going on here?"

"Who are you?" I blurted out.

"I came to look at this house," he snapped. "It's for sale, you know. Will you please tell me what's going on?"

"There's a body upstairs. In the bedroom closet."

He let me go and stared, first at me, then up the stairs.

"What did you say? A body? Of a person?"

I bit back the remark that almost escaped and nodded. His thoughts weren't hard to follow as he looked back at me, took a deep breath and squared his shoulders. A man about to take charge.

"Here, you go on down and stay with Bernice, my wife. I'll be right back."

A little more shoulder squaring and he disappeared up the stairs. I was more than willing to follow orders, for the moment, and joined the softly moaning Bernice.

"Oh, oh, my God, a dead person, oh my," she kept repeating between sniffles. There was another tissue in my pocket and I offered it to her, hoping Harvey would hurry. It didn't take him long. He came down the stairs, one hand on the banister, the other over his mouth, his face the color of vanilla pudding.

"She's right," he told his wife, "there's a dead man in the closet. He's covered in blood."

"Who is he?" she whispered from behind her wadded-up tissue.

"How would I know?" he retorted, then turned to me. "Who is he?"

"I don't know," I said. "I found him when I was turning on lights for... Are you the people who called Harper's Land Sales?"

Harvey nodded.

"I'm your real estate agent," I said.

Harvey didn't look reassured at that announcement. Bernice sniffled again.

"We have to do something, get the police," Harvey told us. "Someone had better stay here, though. You—" he pointed at me "—you and Bernice go find a phone. I'll stay."

Bernice didn't think much of that idea. She shied away from me and clung to Harvey, turning her moaning up a notch.

"Oh, Harvey, I don't think… I just couldn't drive…. My nerves…"

"Bernice, pull yourself together. This young lady'll drive. Won't you?"

He propped Bernice up by grabbing her elbow, then looked at me hopefully. She winced, frowned, and then sagged against him a little more.

"You go call," I said. "Take Bernice with you. I'll stay here." Staying in that house couldn't be worse than going with Bernice.

"You sure?" He looked doubtful for a second and Bernice sagged some more. He tightened his grip on her elbow and pushed her out the front door.

"We won't be long," he called.

I watched them race toward their car and roar off down the street. Maybe he was afraid I'd change my mind.

The house was filled with silence, making me a lot more nervous than I'd wanted to let on to Harvey. The rain had stopped for a moment, and, out the living room window, I could clearly see the truck. Did it belong to the man upstairs? What was he doing here? There was a logo on the truck door, which seemed familiar. I strained to make out the letters, but it was too far away.

I thought about the man. Was he who I suspected? Should I find out?

"Absolutely not!" My words sounded too loud in the still room, and they didn't have much effect. I knew what I was going to do.

Once more up the stairs, slowly, trying this time to make each step silent. There was no one to hear me coming, but noise somehow seemed wrong. I tiptoed to the bedroom, stood in the open door and forced myself to walk to the closet and look in. Harvey hadn't turned off the light, and I knew I was going to get a full view. Finally, one deep breath, one large step, and I was in front of it.

The man had been tall, with full, wavy blond hair turned to silver. Now it was matted with blood. Blood seemed to be everywhere. It had dripped over one eye, down the crease by his nose and onto his mustache, turning the blond tip of it red. There were splashes on the wall and over the tarp. Tarp? For the first time I noticed he was lying not on bare floor, but on a big canvas painter's tarp. It was thrown over his legs and the lower part of his body. He was lying on his left side, almost on his stomach, with only half his face visible, but it was enough.

The slam of a car door broke the spell. In the distance, sirens screamed. I ran for the stairs and reached the bottom as the front door opened and Harvey appeared. He looked at me trying not to pant and said, "You all right?"

"Fine," I replied. "Where's Bernice?"

"In the car. Says she never wants to set foot in this house again."

Really. What a surprise.

Several police cars and a fire truck careened into the street. Their sirens died, but their lights kept turning. The reflection through the living room windows turned the walls a soft red, sickeningly reminiscent of the upstairs closet. I stayed in the entry hall.

The first policeman through the door was middle-aged and needle thin.

"You the folks that called?" The words were clipped, his voice monotone.

Harvey nodded.

"Where's the body?"

I pointed up the stairs. "Master bedroom. The one with the fireplace. He's in the closet."

The policeman looked at me, opened his mouth to say something, but was distracted as the entry hall filled with uniformed men. Several looked around uncertainly, a couple favored us with curious looks. The thin one immediately took charge.

"You, Gary, take these people into the kitchen, or someplace out of our way, and get their statements. Don't let them touch anything. The rest of you, up here."

The police trooped upstairs, followed by two paramedics, carrying black emergency kits.

"A little late for them, isn't it?" I asked. No one answered.

Gary motioned to us. We followed him, Harvey hanging back, casting furtive glances up the staircase. Curiosity is a powerful thing.

The kitchen was bright under its luminous ceiling. I looked around, wishing there was someplace to sit down. The countertop looked inviting but I discarded that idea almost immediately and leaned instead. There was a clipboard under my elbow. My fingers somehow seemed to fall on top of it and I turned it around so I could read the logo.

"What's that," said Harvey, reaching for it.

"Excuse me," said Gary. He pulled the clipboard away from him and gave me a shy smile. "That might be evidence."

I hoped not. It was collecting an impressive set of fingerprints.

Gary unzipped his jacket, pulled out a crisp new notebook and fished around in an inside pocket for a pencil. I couldn't help staring at him. Tall, hands and feet still a little big for the rest of him, carrot-colored hair, earnest hazel eyes—and freckles! He didn't look any older than my daughter, Susannah, who was a freshman at UC Santa Barbara. A baby!

He looked up and caught me. Color started to slide up his neck and around his ears, onto his cheeks.

"Something wrong, ma'am?"

"No, no. Nothing," I stammered, embarrassed.

He looked back down at his notebook, cleared his throat, gave me one more uncertain glance and began.

"If you could tell me what you were doing when you found…uh…the body.… Him?"

"I can hardly wait to hear that answer." The voice came from behind me. I swung around to face a tall man with light brown hair, lightly peppered with gray. A neat, sandy-colored mustache topped his mouth, his intensely blue eyes laughed at me.

"Who—no—it can't be. Dan? Daniel Boone Dunham?"

"It can, and it is. How are you, Ellie?"

"But…" I continued to stammer. "Where did you come from?"

I didn't get an answer. A uniformed policeman appeared and said, "Coroner's here, Chief. He wants to talk to you."

The laughter in Dan Dunham's eyes faded. "Be right there. Gary, be sure to get full statements. We'll get them typed later and they can sign them tomorrow. Don't forget to get his—" he nodded at Harvey "—address and phone number. Her, I know where to find."

Dan started to leave, but turned back when I blurted out, "Chief?"

"Of police, right here in Santa Louisa," he agreed.

"You can't be," I exclaimed.

"Why not?"

"Because you were going to teach history in some big university," I said, still staring at him as if he were an apparition from another world.

"Things change, Ellie. Now, please cooperate with this young man, and then go home. Someone will be in touch later."

"I didn't know his middle name was Boone," said Gary, looking at the now empty doorway.

"It's not," I said, staring transfixed at the same place.

"How does he know where to find you?" asked Harvey.

"We grew up next door to each other," I told him, wondering the same thing. I had been back in Santa Louisa a full two weeks and not once had anyone mentioned Dan's name. What was he doing back in this town where he'd vowed never to return, and how did he get to be Chief of Police? Evidently he knew I'd moved back into my parents' house while they tried out retirement in Scottsdale, but how? More important, why hadn't he called, or come to see me? We'd been best friends all during our childhood. Didn't that at least merit a phone call?

Gary, standing with pencil poised, interrupted my rambling thoughts. Harvey was equally as eager to get his answers out of the way and escape to Bernice. Everyone to their own tastes.

The statements didn't take long; there wasn't much to say. I tried to linger in the entry hall but Harvey pushed me out the door in front of him, and I found myself in my car, threading through police cars, fire engines and an ambulance.

I tried to concentrate on driving as I crossed the bridge over the Salinas River back into the old part of town. It was there Dan and I had grown up and where I now lived and worked. This Sunday had started out peacefully enough. It was my first day at the office to answer the phones, to handle clients who might walk in. Sharon Harper and I had picked it because we thought it would be quiet. I could take plenty of time with anyone who called. Sharon had been there in the early afternoon, beautifully dressed for a listing appointment in a soft green wool dress. Nicole Chambers, more informal in slacks and a sweater, had stayed to give me advice, and her husband, Tom, looking downright disreputable in jeans, a sweatshirt and filthy tennis shoes, was in and out. A nice, quiet afternoon for learning. Instead, I got my first clients, immediately lost them, discovered Dan Dunham, and a dead body.

My foot pushed on the accelerator and I headed for home a little faster than rain-slicked streets safely allowed. I knew who the dead man was, and that meant I needed to make a phone call.

THREE

THE WHEELS SLIPPED a little on the old concrete driveway, but I got the car into the garage, pushed the doors shut and entered the house through the back porch. Slipping out of my damp shoes, I threw my jacket over the washing machine, and headed for the phone.

"Sharon," I said. "Something's happened that I think you should know about."

"Oh?" was the only response I got. Cool, reserved, Sharon Harper was going to wait until all the facts were in before committing to a comment.

"You know the new house you have listed? The one on Morning Glory Lane? Well, I showed it this afternoon."

"That's fine, Ellen." Left unsaid, but obvious in her tone, was—*and?*

"Sharon, I found a body. A dead man, in the upstairs closet."

There was a long pause. "Say that again."

"A dead body, Sharon. The police are there now."

"A dead body." There was another long pause. "In my listing?"

"Yes, and I think…"

"Do you know who it—ah…"

"I think it's that contractor, Hank Sawyer. Isn't he your client?"

"Hank—are you sure?"

"Pretty sure," I told her. I didn't blame her for being incredulous. It was hard to believe, even for me who'd found him.

"And the police are there now?" she went on, in the same flat tone of shock.

"As we speak. They took my statement and sent me home. Listen, Sharon, shouldn't we do…"

"Ellen, I'm coming over." Now she sounded like the decisive Sharon I worked for. "You need to tell me everything. Good God. Hank Sawyer. I have several of his houses listed." The phone went dead.

Damn. Hank Sawyer was a friend of Sharon's, one of the town's most prominent contractors, and an important client. I'd thought it only right to tell her what had happened, but hadn't expected her to rush over here. Now I'd have to do something. Offer her coffee? A sandwich? Nothing I'd read in *Miss Manners* covered anything quite like this. Wine. I'd open a bottle of wine. But first I was getting out of this wool skirt and shedding both bra and panty hose. Sweats, tube socks, moccasins and a fire were going to happen, in that order.

The doorbell rang as I sat an open bottle of

local chardonnay and two glasses on the round coffee table between my two long sofas. Sharon had made good time. Only it wasn't Sharon.

"Surprise, Ellen." Nicole bounced into the room, waving a brown paper bag at me. Tom was right behind her, pushing his glasses back up on his nose, grinning broadly.

"We brought you a bottle of wine to celebrate your first showing," Nicole said. "Where's your opener? What a great fire, just what we need on a night like this."

"Ah—there's one on the table," I said. "I'll get a couple of glasses."

"I'll get them," Tom offered. He handed me his coat and Nicole's. I hung them on pegs in the entry, and followed them back into the living room.

"We're only going to stay a minute," Nicole said, pulling the wine from the bag, "just long enough for a toast, but we couldn't let a momentous event like your first clients pass by without a little celebration. Besides, we wanted to know how everything went."

"Glasses are in the kitchen," I told Tom. I took the sack from Nicole, wadded it up and placed it on the fire. Celebrating was not in order. As to how things went? Not wonderful.

Tom turned toward the kitchen door, his shoe scuffed on my wood floor, and he stumbled.

"Serves you right for buying such ugly shoes," Nicole told him.

"Only ones I could find on a Sunday," he replied. "Besides, they're not so bad."

"They're hideous," she called after him. "Why he had to buy shoes today I'll never know." She worked the cork out of the bottle of merlot. "The only place open on Sunday is the new little shop those Indian brothers run over on Peach. Tom could have waited until tomorrow."

"And gone to the Emporium," he finished. "There are so many choices in this town."

Nicole laughed, took the glasses and started to fill them. "Were you expecting someone, Ellen?" She indicated the extra glass on the table. "We don't want to interrupt."

"Sharon's coming," I said.

"Sharon?"

Tom's eyebrows went up in surprise. "I didn't know you were friends."

"We aren't," I replied. "That is, we are, but not really. Anyway, that's not why she's coming. Something happened this afternoon. I called her and…"

The doorbell rang again, cutting me off.

"Sit down," I said. "That's her, and you might as well hear all this now as later."

"Oh." Sharon paused in the doorway, eyeing

Tom and Nicole. "I didn't know Ellen had called you also."

"She didn't," Nicole told her. "We came by to celebrate her first clients. Evidently something happened? Ellen was about to tell us."

Sharon examined the two warm-up jackets hanging in my entry, then looked dispassionately at all of us. Tom was in jeans, an old UCLA sweatshirt and the new, truly ugly running shoes. Nicole had on leggings, UGG boots and a baggy sweater. They suited her small body and tangled mop of bronze curls. All five-foot-six of me was wrapped in bright red sweats, adding considerable bulk to my size-ten frame. My light brown hair, which frizzed in rain instead of curling, I'd pulled back off my face with combs. We did not look like business professionals. Sharon, however, was dressed in a trim navy blue suit, white silk blouse, navy low-heeled pumps and panty hose. Poor thing.

I hung her wool coat on a hanger in the entryway closet and followed her into the living room. She was already seated on one end of a sofa, looking slightly out of place against its flowered chintz background. She reached up to take the glass of wine Tom offered.

"Ellen hasn't told you?" she said.

"Ellen hasn't said anything, but maybe she

should," Tom said, picking up his own glass. "This is beginning to sound ominous. Do we hold the toast for a while?"

"I'm afraid so." I sighed, then sank down in the easy chair that faced the fire and them and started my story. It got quite a reaction.

Tom set his glass down on the table with a small bang. Nicole's was motionless, halfway between the table and her face.

"Good God, Ellen. You really think the man was murdered?" Tom said.

"I can't think of any other reason for him to be in that closet with blood all over everything," I replied. There was shakiness in my voice I couldn't quite control.

"I can't believe we let you go on that appointment alone," Tom said. "I'm so sorry."

"Don't be silly," I told him, my voice a little too loud, but stronger. It's amazing how brave you can be with an audience. "It's not the kind of thing you can predict."

"True," Tom said, with a hint of a smile. "It's a first."

"I hope it's a last," I said somewhat tartly.

"Oh, Ellen, how awful." Nicole's hazel eyes were wide and round. Her glass finally made it to her mouth, she took a sip, and then asked, "Do you know who the man was?"

"She thinks she does," Sharon put in.

"I'm pretty sure it was that contractor you introduced me to yesterday, Hank Sawyer," I said.

Nicole choked.

I started out of my chair. "Are you all right?" I asked.

"Yesterday?" Tom turned so he was looking directly at Nicole. "I told you…"

Nicole waved me away. "Fine, I'm fine," she said, gasping for breath a little. She turned toward Tom, ignoring Sharon and me. "Did you hear what she said? Were you listening? Hank Sawyer is dead. Murdered. Hank Sawyer. Someone killed him."

The angry red flush that had crept up Tom's face started to fade. He looked from Nicole, to me, then at Sharon, finally back to Nicole. "Oh, my God," he said.

I had no idea what was going on. The two of them were sitting on my sofa, looking like I'd taken a poleax to them.

"I didn't realize you and Hank Sawyer were such close friends," I said. "I'm sorry if I shocked you."

Nicole gave a brittle little laugh. "*Shock* is a good word." She drained the wine in her glass, and then got up. "We've got to go. I'm sorry today was so—awful, Ellen. I really am. Come on, Tom. We'll see you tomorrow, Sharon."

Tom had been staring into his glass. He held it up, looked at the remaining dull red wine, shuddered, and put it down. "I'm sorry too, Ellen. Sorry you had to go through that and, well, everything. Sharon, oh, damn it all. We'll see you both tomorrow I guess."

He took their jackets off the pegs, handed Nicole hers, and, without looking back, walked out.

FOUR

THEY HADN'T GIVEN me time to get out of my chair. "I'm beginning to have great sympathy for Alice down the rabbit hole," I said, reaching for the merlot. "What just happened?"

Sharon took the bottle from me, examined the label, rejected it and reached for the chardonnay. There were little frown wrinkles between her eyebrows. Black lashes framed light brown eyes that had lost their usual confident look. She took a deep breath before she answered me. "I'm afraid this is going to get messy."

"Going to!" I exclaimed. "There's a dead man in a closet of a house you have listed, he was your client and, I thought, your friend. Isn't that messy enough?"

"I'd better tell you about Hank," Sharon said slowly. "It's hard to say without making him seem—raunchy. He wants—wanted—I really can't believe any of this is happening—anyway, Hank is—oh dear, was—the original good ol' boy. The kind who makes slightly dirty jokes, tells you how sexy you look, then lets his hands roam if you don't stop him. Most women are embarrassed and don't know what to say. Hank thought that meant they liked his little attentions and kept going. Occasionally he found someone who really wanted to play."

"Umm," I said. "Unfortunately, that didn't make him unique. What's that got to do with Tom and Nicole? Unless…?"

"Yes. He'd started in on Nicole. She's young, wasn't sure how to handle it. Tom wasn't amused and, a couple of days ago, he lost his temper. He grabbed Hank by the shirtfront and told him to keep his, well, his hands off Nicole. I had to intervene. Hank was a good client. He bought all his lots through me, and sold all his houses through our office. I couldn't afford to have some hot-tempered agent lose me that kind of business."

"Nicole couldn't have thought Tom would do something drastic like killing him, though. Could she?" I asked.

"I don't know what Nicole thought," Sharon said, "but Tom has a terrible temper. I imagine he'll get asked a lot of questions. Now, I've got some. Did the police…"

The doorbell rang. It was busier around here than Macy's on sale day.

"Hi," he said, filling the whole doorway. "Aren't you going to ask me in?"

"I suppose so," I said, and stepped back a little.

"You don't look pleased to see me," Dan said, hanging his jacket on a peg the same way he used to. "How long's it been, Ellie? Over twenty years, anyway. You're looking good."

"What did you expect? Gray hair and rolls of fat?"

"I see the years haven't improved your disposition much. That merlot looks nice. Glasses in the kitchen?"

Dan grinned at Sharon, who wiggled fingers back at him, pushed open the swinging door into the kitchen and returned immediately with a glass, which he proceeded to fill.

"The place looks great, Ellie. Better than I remembered." He lowered himself onto the sofa across from Sharon. "These weren't here before," he said, patting the flowered print. "Neither was that table. Same bookshelves, though. You need to stir the fire."

I poked the logs with a little more force than necessary, then retired to my easy chair. "Is this call social or business?" I asked in my nastiest tone.

"My, you are thorny," Dan said. "A little of each. Sharon, I'm glad you're here. I've got a couple of questions for you. Save me the trouble of stopping by your place."

Sharon looked surprised, but I didn't give her a chance to say anything.

"Listen, Daniel Boone Dunham." Dan winced at the "Boone," which didn't bother me a bit. "Before we go any further, there are a couple of questions I want answered. Where did you come from? How did you get to be Chief of Police? And why were you so darn cold this afternoon? You were nice for about thirty seconds, and then you turned into an ice bucket. And why haven't you been over to see me before now?"

"Is that why you're so mad?" he said with a little smile.

"Of course not," I said, using my most dignified tone. "And I'm not mad."

"You could have fooled me. Anyway, I'll catch you up on my past history later. I've even got a few questions for you. This afternoon, well, I'm a policeman, with a job to do. It wasn't the time for a chat." He paused, looked at me over the top of his glass, then looked down, hiding the expression in his eyes before he went on. "I've been meaning to come over, thought I'd let you settle in first. I never expected—anyway, I'm here now." He looked up and grinned. My old playmate was back. Dan, who'd been better than a brother, who...

"Never mind all that. Tell us what happened,

Dan," Sharon said. "Was it really Hank Sawyer? Do you know who did it?"

"It really was Hank and no, not yet. We're investigating."

I gave a snort. Dan ignored me.

"What happened?" Sharon repeated. "Every time I ask Ellen for any details, we get interrupted."

We weren't going to this time. I also wanted to know what had happened.

"What was he hit with?" I asked. "It must have been something pretty hard, there was an awful lot of blood."

"Head wounds bleed a lot," Dan said noncommittally.

"Dan—" I started.

"We think whoever it was used a brick, one of the ones by the upstairs fireplace. It looks like he was attacked in the bedroom, pulled into the closet while lying on the tarp, then hit a few more times."

I felt a little sick. Sharon's face was blank but she'd turned pale under her makeup.

"Who would do such a thing?" I blurted out.

"That's what we mean to find out," Dan said, then turned his attention to Sharon again. "Wasn't Hank a client of yours?" he asked.

Sharon nodded.

"He was in and out of your office a lot," Dan

pressed, making it more a statement than a question. Sharon nodded again.

"I hear there's been some problems lately," Dan went on.

Here we go, I thought. *Poor Tom.*

Sharon looked up, started to say something, but changed her mind. "Hank was going to press some kind of charges against Ray Yarbourough?" Dan went on.

I sat up straight. Ray? I hadn't heard that. Ray was the only other agent at Harper's Land Sales. I didn't like him much, but couldn't see him bashing Hank over the head. He wouldn't want to get blood on his white shoes.

"Hank said something, yes," Sharon answered carefully, not looking at Dan. "We had a meeting set for tomorrow afternoon, the three of us."

"What did Hank think Ray had done?"

"I don't know." Sharon sighed. She looked directly at Dan for the first time. "I didn't want to know. I told Hank to bring in his information, or proof, or whatever. I'd let Ray answer, then we'd see."

"Hmm," Dan said, then started to pat his pockets. He stood up, patted some more, and headed for his jacket.

"What are you doing?" I asked.

"Getting this," he answered. He handed Sharon

a piece of stationery with a Harper's Land Sales logo. "Ever seen this before?"

My curiosity was itching like crazy. I got up and went behind Sharon to try to read what was on that paper. Nothing but a list of names and addresses.

"We found that in Hank's pocket. Couldn't help but wonder about it," Dan went on. "See, some of the names have yellow highlighter, others don't. Hank's on that list, and his name isn't highlighted. Neither is yours, Sharon."

"Where did you get this?" Sharon asked. She stared down at it, holding it in two fingers as though it might explode.

"I told you," Dan said mildly. "Hank's pocket. It's a list of—what?"

"These are the original investors in a limited partnership I put together, oh, a couple of years ago," she said slowly. "We bought land. Just one piece of land. The highlighted names sold their shares, the others are still in."

"What land?" Dan asked, holding out his hand for the paper.

Sharon took a deep breath, hesitated a minute, and finally handed it to him. "The land Stop N Shop is buying to build their new store," she said.

"Holy—Toledo," Dan said. "Everybody thought that land was worthless, until Stop N Shop came to town. You all must have made a killing."

"It's turned out quite well," she said. A brief satisfied smile came and went, replaced by a frown. "At least financially. There are times when I wish I'd never heard of Stop N Shop."

"Why?" I asked. "It's exactly what this town's been needing for years. We've always had to go to San Luis Obispo to shop, unless you wanted to brave the Emporium. Everyone must be delighted."

"Not everyone," Sharon said. "There are a lot of people who don't think that store should come. They're being led by Benjamin Lockwood and they all blame me."

"Benjamin Lockwood," I mused, lost for a moment in the past. "I haven't thought about him in years. Does he still run the Emporium?"

"He does," Sharon said with a grimace. "Which is part of the problem."

"I used to love the Emporium," I went on. "How could…"

"Later, Ellie, later," Dan interrupted, sitting forward a little. "Sharon, wasn't there some kind of ruckus recently between old Benjamin and Hank?"

"There was. Right in front of my office," Sharon said. Her lips pursed, and her fingers tightened a little around her glass. "Hank was leaving and Benjamin rushed up to him, hollering and waving his arms, saying Hank was a traitor, in league with me, and he should give up his seat on the Planning Commission."

"That's a bit strong," Dan commented. He nodded at Sharon to go on. "What did Hank say?"

"You know Hank. He never took anything very seriously. He laughed, then told Benjamin that he wasn't going to vote on the Stop N Shop plans or on conditions for the new store because he was a partner in the corporation." Sharon paused, absently twirled the wine glass in her fingers and watched the wine swirl. "Unfortunately, he went on to say that if Benjamin was worried about Stop N Shop ruining the Emporium, he shouldn't. Benjamin was doing a fine job of that all by himself. That's when Benjamin grabbed a hammer out of Hank's truck and attacked him with it."

Dan started to smile. "I heard about that. Benjamin stormed into the station, wanting to file something, anything, against Hank. He wasn't too happy when my officer told him the attacker couldn't file charges. I gather he didn't do Hank any damage."

"No." Sharon shook her head. "Hank took the hammer away from him, threw it in the back of his pickup, and left Benjamin sputtering on the sidewalk."

She paused a minute, glanced at Dan, looked

away, and went on, "Benjamin was pretty explicit about what he'd do to Hank if he got the chance."

"You don't seriously think old Benjamin Lockwood could have killed Hank, do you?" I exclaimed. "Why, he was older than dirt when we were all growing up. Besides, he wouldn't!"

"He wasn't as old as we all thought," Dan said, running his fingers through his hair, just like he used to when he couldn't get a math problem to come out right.

"Things aren't what they used to be, Ellen." Sharon had on her serious face, the one she used in the office. "Or maybe, when we were children, we saw things differently. Benjamin's always been a little strange and ever since Rose died, he's been— well, stranger. And he's tough. I'm not saying he did it, but I'll bet he could have."

"I don't believe it," I protested. "Nobody we know would do such a thing. I'll bet it was a thief or something. Dan, don't you think so?"

"Mighty sloppy thief," he commented. "Hank's wallet wasn't touched and the keys to the pickup were in the ignition."

"Maybe he was scared off," I said, not willing to give up my easy solution so quickly.

"By who?" Dan sounded curious, as though he was willing to explore my theory. Then he ruined it all. "Hank's is the only house on that street close to being finished. You, Bernice and Harvey were the only ones who were there today. Except, of course, the murderer."

I didn't like that much. I didn't like Dan's grin much either. I was trying to think of something, anything, when I saw Sharon's face. She was staring at one of the bookshelves that flanked the fireplace.

"Is that a cat?" she gasped. Her face was white, her tone strangulated.

"That's Jake," I said, wondering why she looked so strange. "Handsome, isn't he?"

Jake, my big yellow tom, was sitting on the top shelf, shining up his white feet and bib in preparation for dinner. Dan set down his glass and started to his feet. So did I.

"Watch this," I told them, and whistled. Jake quit bathing, stood up, stretched, then sailed off the shelf to land on the back of the sofa where Sharon sat. She screamed, and threw her hands up over her face.

"Take it away, please, I can't—get rid of it!"

The panic in her voice was real. I grabbed Jake, who howled in protest, looked at Dan, who was making shooing motions with his hands, and headed for the kitchen with the cat in my arms.

"I don't think you were a hit," I told him. He

investigated his empty dish, and made soft complaining noises.

"I had no idea Sharon was afraid of cats. You could get me fired, did you think of that? Then where would your dinner come from?" I opened a can, filled his dish and put it on the floor. He ignored me and started to eat.

"Do you realize everything I've done or touched today has gone wrong?" was my parting comment. The tip of his tail twitched, but I didn't think it was in sympathy for me. I closed the kitchen door so Jake couldn't make a reappearance and returned to the living room.

Sharon was sitting on the other sofa, looking better. Dan was hovering over her.

"I'm so sorry, Sharon. I would never have whistled him down if I'd known," I said.

"It's all right, Ellen," she replied. Her voice sounded controlled and almost normal. "I'm the one who should apologize. For some reason I've never been able to overcome this. Such a silly thing." She fingered the buttons on her jacket, found they were all intact, and unfolded her shapely legs. "It's been a hard day," she continued, with a little sigh, "the news about Hank and all. I guess the shock of seeing the cat was too much. Anyway, I think I'd like to go home. Dan, was there anything else?"

"No, and if there is, I know where to find you," he said. He followed her into the entryway, helped her on with her coat, opened the door for her, flicked on the porch light although it wasn't quite dark, and waited until she was down the stairs before coming back toward the living room, the fire, and me.

"Are you all right?" he asked as he picked up his glass and sat back down. I was feeling pretty strung out, especially after the episode with Sharon, and I guess it showed. "What happened this afternoon, that was a tough thing to see, even for a cop." There was sympathy in Dan's voice, which immediately made me feel better.

"It wasn't fun," I agreed, "but I think I'm over the shock." I shuddered. "But I hope I never find another body."

"It's like lightning," Dan said, smiling a little. "It doesn't usually strike twice."

"Good," I said, and was suddenly struck dumb. I kept looking at this Dan, sitting there, an over-grown version of the boy I'd grown up with. The one who'd shared all of my holidays, taught me to swim, and later, to drive, who'd made a fort in my backyard, then wouldn't let me in it, who'd... This wasn't that Dan. This was a strange man, a very good-looking strange man. My Dan didn't have silver sprinkled into his sandy hair, or a neat little mustache, and he didn't have worry lines around his intensely blue eyes. This was a policeman, come to ask me questions about a murder, and I was suddenly wildly uncomfortable.

"Hey, Ellie," Dan said, putting his glass down on the round coffee table and leaning toward me. "You still in there?"

"What?" I said, looking everywhere but at him. "What are you talking about?"

"You look a little nervous, or something. Are you sure you're okay?"

"Of course," I said with as much dignity as I could. I unfolded my red sweat-suit-covered legs, thought of Sharon's silky clad ones, vowed to throw these old things in the trash and headed for the kitchen, wondering if he'd follow.

FIVE

HE DID. He BROUGHT both wine bottles into the kitchen, along with the dirty glasses, put them in the sink. He leaned against the doorjamb, watching me.

"I'm going to make a sandwich." I opened the refrigerator and peered in. "Want one?"

"Sure," Dan said.

"Pour yourself some more wine."

"One glass is all for me," he said, still watching me. "I don't suppose you could make coffee?"

"Probably." I was still staring at the shelves, wondering why I felt so strange.

"Aren't you getting a little cold?"

"What?" I whirled around, ready to be defensive. "Why do you…" There stood the old Dan, back again. He could have been twelve, but he watched me out of over-forty eyes. It was disconcerting.

"I'm looking for stuff. Ham, cheese, tomato, lettuce, mayo, on wheat. Okay?"

"You remembered." He straightened up. "Move over. You never did know how to slice a tomato."

I made coffee, Dan constructed the sandwiches. Followed closely by Jake, we carried everything back into the living room. This time Dan stirred the fire.

"Wonderful." He took a huge bite and fed Jake a piece of cheese, glanced at me, but said nothing more until his sandwich was gone. "I was starved," he told me unnecessarily. He picked up his coffee cup, sipped and settled back, this time taking a long look at me.

"This wasn't how I pictured us getting reacquainted, Ellie. I had it all planned. I'd come by, bring champagne, you'd be surprised but delighted, and we'd spend a quiet evening catching each other up on the last twenty years."

"You surprised me." I put down the ruins of my own sandwich. "On the whole, it was a surprising afternoon."

"That I can believe," Dan said a little wryly. "Listen, Ellie, I don't have much time. I have to get back, but I need to ask you some questions."

"Do police chiefs usually make house calls?" I started to feel tense again.

"You're a special case," he told me with the old Dan grin. It faded too quickly. "Now, tell me exactly what happened. Start from when you left your office and try not to leave anything out."

I stared at him for a minute and thought back.

The rain starting as I crossed the bridge, the door refusing to open, finding that it was unlocked, seeing the truck in the side yard but no other car anywhere, turning on the lights, going upstairs, and, finally, looking in the closet. I took Dan through it all, including Bernice's hysterics.

"She didn't see anything, and she acted worse than anyone," I finished. I thought about Hank's body lying in the closet, the blood on the walls, and gave an involuntary shudder.

Dan leaned over and gave my hand a little pat. "You're holding up great, Ellie. I'm proud of you," he said softly. Then he sat back and proceeded to look like a policeman again. The man was worse than a chameleon.

"Did you know Hank Sawyer?"

"I met him yesterday," I told him. "He came in the office looking for Sharon. Nicole introduced me. She made him sound like a pretty important client."

"I think he was more than that. Do you know anything about the Stop N Shop controversy?"

"Not really," I admitted. "There was something in the paper but I didn't read it. Getting here, moving in, starting a new job—there's been so much, I haven't paid any attention."

"You've gone through a lot." There was sympathy in his eyes. "I heard about your divorce. I'm sorry."

I didn't say anything for a moment. I couldn't. How did he know? Did he also know that Brian had asked for the divorce because one of his affairs had turned serious?

"Thanks," I finally said, "but you don't have to be sorry. I'm not."

I didn't know what else to say. Dan looked like he didn't either. "Well. What about this store?"

"Hank was working with Sharon to get that store approved." There was relief in Dan's voice as he went on. "Being on the city Planning Commission, he was in a position to do some heavy-duty lobbying. I didn't know Sharon and Hank both owned shares in that partnership, though." He looked thoughtful, and abruptly changed the subject. "Tell me what you know about Ray Yarbourough."

"Ray?" Surprised, I put down my coffee. "Nothing. I barely know the man. Why?"

"Hmm. I wondered if there'd been any talk around your office. Seems Hank had told some others that, this time, he was going to get Ray's license. Do you know anything about that?"

"This time?" I asked, startled. "There've been other times?"

"Hank and Ray have—had—a feud that goes way back."

"Oh," I said, then, "Oh! You think Ray might have…"

"I don't think anything yet. I hear Hank was starting in on Nicole Chambers. That true?"

"You hear a lot," I answered, somewhat tartly.

"There's been a murder," Dan said mildly. "That means we have to ask questions. Most of them lead nowhere, but we still have to ask."

There was nothing in Dan's statement or tone to upset me. It did anyway.

"I don't know these people," I said. "I've only been at Harper's a week. I met Hank Sawyer one time, and he acted just fine."

I looked at Dan, sitting quietly on the sofa, stroking Jake, and decided I was overdefensive and didn't know why. "Ray Yarbourough is a jerk, though," I offered a little weakly.

Dan laughed. "You won't get any argument from me. No one said anything about Hank and him?"

"Not around me," I said. "I only met Hank once, and didn't know anything about him until Sharon told me. And I had no idea our office was handling the sale of land to Shop N Stop, or that a few people objected to it."

"Try half the town," Dan said. He put Jake

down, stretched and got to his feet. "I've got to go. Thanks for the sandwich." He took his coat off the peg, slipped into it, reached for the door handle, but turned back.

"What are you doing tomorrow?" he said.

"Working."

"You'll need to give us a formal statement. I'll pick you up at your office about eleven. That'll give you plenty of time before we go to lunch."

The door closed and he was gone, leaving a bushel basket of questions behind. Dan was taking me to lunch? Just like that? What happened to asking? And what was all this about Stop N Shop? What could a new store possibly have to do with Hank's murder? Unless Sharon was right and Benjamin Lockwood—no. Absolutely not.

Ray Yarbourough? Did Hank know something that threatened Ray so much he had to kill to protect himself? Of course not. Ray was my worst image of a salesman, pushy, always talking about the close, but I couldn't see him as a crook, and certainly not as a murderer.

I didn't believe for one minute that Tom Chambers could do something as barbaric as beat Hank to death with a brick. I'd never seen anything but an easygoing young man. But he was obviously in love with his bubbly little wife. Did he have a violent streak? I didn't think so.

No. Whoever was responsible wasn't someone I knew or had ever met. I got up and went into the kitchen, looked at the merlot bottle, corked it and put it on the rack, then poured more coffee, added a little flavored creamer and went back into the living room to give the fire another poke. I turned on the TV but didn't watch it. There were a couple of other questions that kept repeating themselves, over and over. Why was Dan back in Santa Louisa? Why, and when, had he become a policeman? One more question kept sneaking in, one I wanted to ignore, but couldn't. Was there a Mrs. Dunham?

SIX

MONDAY MORNING CAME too soon. I stood at my kitchen window, sipping my first cup of coffee, watching a brisk breeze blow the remaining clouds away, and yawned. It had taken a while to get to sleep last night and an awesome nightmare hadn't helped. Hank's dead body, stuffed in the closet, had reappeared. A shadowy figure was behind him and this time I was the target. I was fleeing down the stairs, the shadow right behind me, when I woke up. I spent the next hour or so with the light on. Bravery is a relative thing.

I was rinsing my coffee cup, ready to head for the shower, when the phone rang.

"Mom," said a plaintive voice, one I knew well. "What's going on over there? You're on the news. They said you found a dead body. Did you?"

"Hello, Susannah," I said to my daughter. "Yes, I did."

"Why?"

Now there was an unanswerable question.

"It wasn't my idea," I told her. "He was there, and unfortunately, so was I."

"The news said he was murdered." Accusation was ripe in her voice.

"He was, but don't worry. I didn't do it."

"Really, Mother. I knew that. But someone did. What if the murderer saw you? You could be in danger. Did you think of that?"

I had. My nightmare proved it, but I wasn't going to share that with Susannah. "There wasn't anyone around. Just me, Harvey and Bernice."

"Who?" Her confusion was understandable. "How about if you start at the beginning and tell me all."

I told her the little I knew, reviewing what Sharon had told me about Tom and Nicole, the feud between Hank and Ray, and the list of names Dan had found in Hank's pocket.

"Mom, that's awful." She said that after she had pulled a detailed description of Hank's body from me. "Are you all right?"

"Still a little shaky," I admitted, "but fine."

"Who's Dan?" Susannah abruptly changed the subject.

"Dan Dunham. He lived next door to me for years, until he went away to college. His parents left town that same year. He turned up yesterday as the Chief of Police."

"Is he cute?" Leave it to youth to get right to the point.

"For heaven's sake, Susannah. He's an old friend, that's all." I said, in my best mother-to-child voice.

"Old friend, right. Did he ask you out?"

"Susannah," was all I could think to say. I didn't mention lunch, but suddenly it loomed large in my mind.

"I've got a class, Mom. Gotta go. Call me tonight?"

"Sure, honey. Be careful."

"I don't need to. You're the one finding dead bodies." She hung up.

I had to laugh a little. How nice Susannah was worried about me. How funny she was thinking of pairing me up with someone other than her father. That thought hadn't crossed my mind.

I glanced at the clock, and came back to reality with a thud. Eight-thirty. I'd better hit the shower and head for the office. I'd never learn to be a real estate agent sitting in my kitchen.

Upstairs, I rummaged through my closet, looking for something to wear. Cords and a sweater? That clear sky promised a chilly day. I caught sight of my red sweats, peeking out of the clothes hamper, and thought about lunch. Out came the new dress I'd been saving for some reason. It was a wonderful shade of blue. If I added a cardigan, I'd be just fine.

"My, Ellen, you look nice." Dottie Fielding, our office secretary, looked up as I came in the door and gave her usual tentative smile.

"Thanks." I smiled back. Dottie ducked her head and let her fingers fly once more over her computer keyboard. I paused for a second, wondering as I had every day since I met her, how someone who seemed so insecure could be so deadly efficient. Messages wouldn't get taken, files would disappear and chaos would reign supreme if it weren't for her, but you wouldn't know it from her appearance. Only in her mid-forties, she seemed determined to look years older. Shapeless clothes, indifferent haircut, sensible shoes my grandmother wouldn't be caught dead in, Dottie was the stereotype of an old maid. I wondered why, but there were other questions more pressing.

"Where is everybody?" I looked around at an almost empty office.

"They're all out on appointments." Almost as an afterthought, as if she was afraid I'd feel bad I didn't have one, she offered, "Nicole's back there, at her desk."

"Thanks," I said again and wandered over toward Nicole. I wasn't sure what to say but she didn't notice my hesitation.

"Ellen, there you are. Your Aunt Mary called."

She looked up at me with tired eyes. Someone else had trouble sleeping last night, I thought.

"Oh? Did she say what she wanted?"

"Something about flowers," Nicole answered a little vaguely.

"Flowers? Flowers for what?"

"Hank's funeral."

"Hank's—why would I send him flowers? I didn't know the man."

It was obvious Nicole didn't care about flowers, who sent them, or if no one did. She looked past me toward the front of the office and Tom. He let the door swing shut, dropped a folder of papers on Dottie's desk, and headed our way.

"I don't know what she meant, Ellen." Nicole pushed back her chair, her eyes firmly on Tom. "Call and ask her."

"Hi, Ellen." Tom barely glanced at me. He took Nicole by the arm and they headed for the coffee machine in the back. Clearly, I wasn't invited.

I watched for a minute, decided any real estate training I'd planned to get from either of them wasn't going to happen today, and checked the clock. Nine-thirty. Plenty of time to visit Aunt Mary before eleven and my appointment at the police station. Lunch, I resolutely pushed out of my mind.

"Dottie, I'll be back at eleven." I tucked my

purse under my arm, and started on the four-block
walk to my Aunt Mary's house.

She is the oldest of my mother's four sisters.
She moved into the house on Chestnut when she
and Uncle Philip were married and, after he died,
saw no reason to move out. I'd spent almost as
much time at her house while growing up as at my
own and Dan had been an equally frequent visitor. We "helped" her make cookies, put up apricot
jam, set out tomato plants and, as we got older,
painted her fence and learned to make an angel
food cake from scratch. At least, I did. She was
the one adult who was never too busy to listen,
so into her ear went complaints about school, big
sisters who teased, Girl Scout badges that refused
to be won, and later, boys who didn't ask me to
the prom. I gradually lost touch with her during
the years of my marriage. Brian, my ex, wasn't
interested in small towns or the people in them.
But now I was back, the old habit of talking things
over with Aunt Mary had returned as well, and
heading her way seemed perfectly natural.

SEVEN

WALKING THROUGH the old residential section of our downtown is like taking a step back in time. The stately Victorians painted pastel colors, with fish scale shingles and steep roofs, are the grande dames. The others, built from the turn of the century to the late thirties, are less imposing but more comfortable to live in. California bungalow, Spanish stucco with real tile roofs, deep-porched farmhouse styles of the early twenties, they are all here. The one thing they have in common is the wide, tree-lined streets and the serene look of homes well kept.

Aunt Mary's is a white frame house with a green roof built sometime in the early twenties. Her front door opens directly from the porch into a large friendly living room. I chose to walk around the side, through the garden gate and down the still damp path, past the soon-to-bloom camellias and the freshly trimmed rose bushes, to enter by the old screened-in back porch. I called out a hello as I walked into the warm kitchen, but stopped abruptly. There was a woman I didn't know, sitting at the kitchen table, drinking coffee with Aunt Mary.

"Oh." I started to back up. "I'm sorry. I should have called."

"Come on in, Ellen." Aunt Mary's chair scraped the old linoleum as she pushed it back. She got to her feet and reached for the coffeepot. "Grab a mug off that rack and sit down. I've been wanting you two to meet."

I smiled a little uncertainly at the woman, took a mug and sat down while Aunt Mary filled it. "Have a cookie." She pushed a full plate my way. "Ellen, this is Pat Bennington. Pat, my niece, Ellen McKenzie. She used to be a Page."

Pat nodded. Page, my maiden name, identified my clan in this small town.

"Ellen's the one who found Hank's body yesterday."

"That must have been horrible for you." Pat Bennington's voice, and eyes, held real empathy. I decided right then I liked her. About my age, soft, reddish brown hair with a hint of gray she hadn't bothered to cover, light brown eyes, remnants of a summer tan that hadn't come from a tube, and she visited my Aunt Mary. Yes, someone I needed to get to know better.

"It was pretty horrible." I gave a little shudder at the memory.

"Humph," was Aunt Mary's response. There was sympathy in her eyes but she wasn't ready to let me talk about it yet. "I've been telling Pat about you. She thinks you should join their Little Theater group. I do, too. You'd love it."

My hand jerked and a little of the coffee spilled. I reached for a napkin to mop it up, thankful that I could hide the horror I knew was on my face. Little Theater. The very thought made me turn cold. But I managed to look up and smile.

"Sounds—interesting," I said. "You'll have to tell me more about it sometime."

Pat looked at me, then at Aunt Mary, and smiled. "Right. We meet at the Veteran's hall. Stop by sometime. Mary, thanks for the coffee, and for listening. I'll talk to you later about—well, I'll talk to you later."

It wasn't until she was out the door that I took my first good look at my aunt. It was a little unsettling. Never a small woman, over the years she'd added more than a pound or two. Age and size hadn't slowed her down. She ran most of the rummage sale charity fundraisers in town, and had as long as memory served. A woman of strong conscience, she felt honor-bound to purchase anything in her size and, of course, since you can't waste good money, to wear it. It makes for some bizarre combinations. Today she had on shocking-pink sweatpants stretched firmly over her behind and an oversize sweatshirt that featured Mickey Mouse. Mickey dancing across her front was not a sight to gladden Disney hearts.

"She seems nice." I ignored her outfit and nodded toward the back door. "What were you telling her about me?"

"Pat's a good woman." Aunt Mary sidestepped the question. "Are you all right? That had to have been terrible for you. Tell me what happened."

I recited my story once more. When I was finished Aunt Mary said with a sigh, "Poor Hank. Who could have done such a thing?"

"I don't know, but there seem to be several candidates. Did you know him?"

"Of course," she answered me, surprised. "Hank and Vera have lived here all their lives. Hank and your father golfed together."

That was news to me. I would have sworn I'd never heard of Hank Sawyer before Saturday when Nicole introduced us. He hadn't acted like he knew me either, but I'd probably changed a little in the last twenty-plus years and my name was no longer Page.

"What do you mean by 'candidates'?" She looked at me quizzically over the top of her coffee mug. "Hank was a man of strong opinions and he had one or two other small problems, but on the whole, he was a very popular man in this town."

"Really?" I put my mug down and let my skepticism show. "I got the impression from what Sharon said that he was a lecherous old guy who couldn't keep his hands to himself."

"That was one of his problems," Aunt Mary admitted a bit wryly. "I never understood how Vera put up with it all these years. She called it flirting; most of us had another name for it. But he was respected as an honest business man, and he really was fun to be around."

"I doubt if Ray Yarbourough thought so." I reached for another cookie. Oatmeal with raisins, just like the ones she used to make when I was growing up. Delicious. "Sharon told Dan Hank was trying to get Ray's real estate license revoked, or something."

Aunt Mary sighed. "I'll bet that was about Emme Murch. So sad."

"Who?" I'd never heard of Emme Murch. Aunt Mary knew everyone in town and, even though I'd grown up here, I was beginning to feel I didn't know anybody.

"Emme Murch. Her husband died a while ago and Emme couldn't cope. She'd never paid a bill, written a check or made a decision in the fifty-or-so years they'd been married. Her kids had all moved away. Nancy, the daughter who lives in Tennessee, came to take Emme home with her and listed the house with Ray. Hank thought Ray had somehow taken advantage of the situation. I never was sure how."

"Do you think he did?" I said that with real interest. I didn't like the idea of working with someone who cheated old ladies, but couldn't believe Sharon would allow that to happen.

"No." Aunt Mary spoke slowly, a little frown starting on her forehead. "I don't, but I have to admit, I wouldn't choose Ray to represent me."

"Do you think he would have killed Hank because of that?"

"Of course not," she said hotly. "What an idea." Only, she didn't look as if she completely rejected the idea. Her eyes narrowed as she thought. "What happens if you lose your real estate license?"

"We went over that in real estate school but I don't remember exactly. I think, though, if it's something as serious as fraud, you never get it back. Besides, fraud could mean jail, couldn't it?"

She frowned again before she started to vigorously shake her head. "No. Ray couldn't have done it."

"No guts?" I suggested.

She looked startled, then started to laugh. "That wasn't what I was thinking, but you've got a point."

"How about Tom Chambers?" I slowly munched another cookie and watching her closely.

"Why? Because of Nicole? I don't think so. Tom was irritated with Hank, but that's not a motive for murder."

"I'm told Tom has a pretty hot temper." I let a hint of a question come through.

Aunt Mary looked exasperated. "People in this town gossip way too much."

"But does he?" I pressed.

"Have a temper?" She looked at me with a little set to her chin. "I've know Tom Chambers and his family for years. He's a good boy, and now he's grown up, he controls himself just fine."

That wasn't much of an answer and I tried again.

"Maybe so, but jealousy can do strange things to people."

"Why would Tom be jealous of Hank? He knew Nicole wasn't interested in him. If you think jealousy's a motive, then Dottie Fielding's a suspect."

I had been thinking about another cookie but that got my attention fast. "Not Dottie Fielding, our office secretary? What does she have to do with Hank?"

Aunt Mary didn't answer. Instead she picked up the almost empty cookie plate, went to the same cookie jar she'd had when I was a child, started to lift the lid, then turned to me and said, "Would you rather have coffee cake?"

"No, nothing." I waved the plate away. "All right, coffee, then. What about Dottie?"

She didn't reply. Instead, she took a cloth and started to polish the old stove. "I'm never going to buy a stove with a griddle on it again. You just can't keep them clean."

"You're never going to buy a new stove, and you might as well give up trying to change the subject and tell me." I watched her shoulders tighten, then went on. "You brought it up, and I'm not going to let it drop."

"I didn't mean to," she said, her back still turned away from me.

"Probably true, but you did, so tell me."

She sat back down, pulled her coffee mug toward her, poured cream into it and stirred. "I hate gossip." She picked up the mug, drank, made a face and put it down. "It's cold," she said, accusingly.

I didn't say anything, just waited.

"Oh, all right. That's what Pat came for, to see if I thought we should do something." She broke off, and looked at me as if she had explained it all. Sure.

"Do something about what?" Now I was the

one exasperated. The time was slipping by but I wanted to know about Dottie.

Aunt Mary sighed, in defeat, I hoped. "Pat belongs to the Little Theater group," she began slowly.

"I know," I said, hoping to hurry this along. "So?"

"So does Dottie." Aunt Mary sighed. "So did Hank Sawyer."

"And?" I wondered if I was beginning to see.

"Hank had lately been paying a lot of attention to Dottie. Whispering, pulling her off to the side, even took her home the other night."

"What about his wife?"

"Vera hated the theater group."

Vera had my sympathy. "I thought Hank was famous for chasing women. What's so strange about him chasing Dottie?" I pictured Dottie in my mind and had the answer to my question.

"Hank liked pretty women." Aunt Mary's lips pursed. "Like Nicole." She looked at me critically. "Or even you."

Gee, thanks, I thought, but got her point. "Dottie's a mouse. A dowdy mouse. I can't believe she even had the courage to join a theater group."

"She doesn't act." Aunt Mary sounded horrified at the thought Dottie might be asked to get up on a stage and say something. "She does all the other stuff, sews costumes, types scripts, paints scenery, that kind of thing."

"So why was Pat worried?"

"Jealousy. Dottie's never had a man pay attention to her since she was jilted by her fiancé years ago. Pat was worried that she might have taken Hank seriously. Hank was getting older. Not so many women wanted to play. Maybe he found Dottie an easy target—an empty house on a quiet Sunday afternoon would be a good place for a, ah, private meeting. If Dottie envisioned a, well, more permanent relationship, and Hank made it clear he had no intention of leaving Vera, just maybe…"

"You're not serious." I sounded incredulous. I was. "Dottie?"

"She wouldn't be the first woman in history," Aunt Mary said grimly.

I pictured various scenarios and started to nod slowly. "Jealousy," I said, "or maybe—wait a minute. If jealousy's a motive, how about his wife? It sounds like she has the best motive of all."

"I'd thought about that," Aunt Mary said, "but Vera's pretty small. I'm not sure she could have done what you described."

"Sure she could," I said, confident I could pin Hank's murder onto a woman I'd never seen. "If she hit him with the brick and knocked him out, she could have easily dragged him into the closet on the tarp. It didn't take strength to finish him off, just determination."

Aunt Mary shuddered. "That's horrible. No, I don't think Vera has the temperament."

I wasn't so sure. I'd been married to a man who cheated on me and there had been a time or two when banging Brian on the head with a brick would have been tempting.

I looked at the clock. "I've got to be back at the office by eleven, but there are a couple of other things I want to ask you."

"Why eleven?"

"Because I have to go to the police station and give a statement. Dan Dunham's picking me up."

"Dan is, is he." She said that softly with a little smile.

"Yes, he is. Why didn't you tell me he was back in town? Do you know what a shock it was to see him yesterday?" I gritted my teeth. All my pent-up frustration, divorce, moving home, finding a dead body, finding Dan, was in my voice.

"I was going to. Dan wanted to come by and see you. Only, I thought you needed a little time. You've had a lot of adjusting to do the last few months. I told him to wait. I couldn't know you'd stumble on a body and Dan at the same time." She sounded defensive, which was good. That meant she was sorry. Maybe.

"What's he doing back here, anyway? Last time I saw him, he was going to major in history and teach at Harvard, or somewhere."

"He met a girl and got married instead." Aunt Mary watched me closely. "Changed his major, and joined the San Francisco police."

I barely heard the last part, but the *girl* and *married* rang through loud and clear.

"Oh." That came out rather faintly. "Do they have a family?"

"They did." Aunt Mary hadn't taken her eyes off me. It was almost as if she was trying to gauge how I would take what she was going to say next. "Dan's wife and son were killed by a drunk driver a few years ago. It was after that he came back here, to become our Chief of Police, and Santa Louisa's most eligible bachelor."

I don't know what I was expecting, but not that. "Oh," I said. Then, "oh." I thought about Susannah and how devastated I would be to lose her. "How terrible. Poor Dan."

"He went through a pretty bad time." Aunt Mary nodded in agreement. "He's perked up some this last year. I think coming home to Santa Louisa was good for him."

I hoped it would have the same therapeutic effect on me. I, too, had lost a mate, only in my case it had been willingly, and I still had my child. I glanced at the clock, and pushed back my chair.

"I'd better get moving. Chief Dunham said he'd be at the office by eleven and I'll just make it," I said. "I wonder if he'll tell me what's going on."

"Don't count on it," Aunt Mary warned me.

"You mean he's not going to fill me in on why Hank had that list of people in his pocket and what the latest word on the street is about Stop N Shop?" I threw that in teasingly, all the while thinking of Dan and his loss, not Dan the policeman. I was startled when Aunt Mary said sharply, "What list? What about Stop N Shop?"

"Didn't I tell you?" I was halfway to the door, but turned to find a worried expression on her face.

"You didn't say anything about Stop N Shop." There was a frown on her face and more than a little concern in her voice. "What does that store have to do with any of this?"

With one eye on the clock I told her about the list, that Hank and Sharon were some of the investors in the land and Benjamin Lockwood had attacked Hank.

"I knew about the investment group." Aunt Mary nodded a little. "Sharon wanted me to put money in that when she formed it. I turned her down. Shows how smart I am. But, Benjamin.

Well, I guess it doesn't surprise me." She said that with a definite sniff. "Benjamin's always been over the edge, and since Rose died, he's been impossible. He's the one responsible for the uproar this town's in over that store. Telling folks how change is going to ruin their lives, run them out of business, destroy the downtown. The man's possessed."

"Will it ruin the downtown?" An image of our lovely tree-shaded town, with its quiet shops and leisurely foot traffic rose to greet me, and I wondered if Benjamin had a point.

"I've no idea, and neither does Benjamin," Aunt Mary said, "but I do know you're going to be late."

One look at the clock proved her right. "Uh-oh." I gave her a wave, and ran for the screen door.

"Don't let it…" Aunt Mary called. Too late. It slammed shut. I grinned as I hurried down the sidewalk. Some things don't change.

EIGHT

THE OFFICE WAS in an uproar. Sharon was ranting about something and didn't pause when I came in the door. Dottie sat immobile at her desk, looking petrified, and Tom and Nicole stood behind Sharon, evidently trying not to laugh. Ray Yarbourough was in Sharon's office doorway, shaking his finger, trying to talk over her.

"I told you that old man was crazy," he said loudly. "Trying to get on the Planning Commission. I thought anybody'd be better than Hank, but not him. You better get over there, Sharon, and put a stop to it."

"What does it look like I'm doing?" Sharon pushed at him. "But I can't do anything until you get your finger out of my face."

Ray stepped back, Sharon edged past him, almost ran me down on her way to the door, and rushed out.

"Who's trying to get on the Planning Commission? Where is Sharon going?" I asked the room at large. "What's going on?"

"Benjamin Lockwood stormed in here a few

minutes ago." Tom grinned wildly and pushed his glasses back up on his nose. "He was yelling and screaming, arms going a mile a minute."

"He looked like a windmill." Nicole laughed out loud.

"He looked crazy." Dottie's eyes were large and her hand trembled a little as she fiddled with a pencil.

"What did he want?" They hadn't explained a thing.

"To tell Sharon he's going to take Hank's seat on the Planning Commission," Ray said grimly, "and that he plans to vote so many restrictions on building a new store that Stop N Shop will give up considering this town." He glared at Tom and Nicole. "And I don't think that's funny."

"Can he do that?" I asked Ray, cutting off a remark that Tom seemed about to make. His grin had turned to a scowl and he'd taken a step forward.

"I don't know." Ray looked past me to scowl right back at Tom. "That's why Sharon's on her way to City Hall, to make sure he doesn't get appointed."

"I'm sorry." I looked at each of them and shook my head. "I still don't understand. Who cares who is on the Planning Commission, and what does that have to do with us? Or Hank? Or anything?"

It was Dottie, quiet little Dottie, who answered. "The Planning Commission is divided almost evenly between those who want Stop N Shop to come, and those who don't. The land is zoned for that kind of store, but if the Commission loads the Stop N Shop people down with lots of expensive conditions, like having to pay for the new bridge and all the stoplights, they may not come. If Benjamin gets on, he'll push for those conditions and kill the deal."

I was beginning to see. "So will Sharon try to get on instead of Benjamin?"

"If she's smart, she will," Ray said, fingering the gold chain around his neck. The small diamond in his pinkie ring flashed, and he moved his hand around so it flashed again, right in my eye. I moved my head and pretended not to notice.

"Sharon can't be on the Commission." Dottie brought my attention abruptly away from Ray and his jewelry. "It wouldn't be ethical."

"Why not?" Ray's smug smile faded and he stuck out his jaw a little. "We need that store, and Sharon should do whatever it takes."

"Dottie's right." Tom pushed his glasses even further up on his nose and eyed Ray with distaste. "It would be a conflict of interest."

"How?" I wondered where all the animosity had so suddenly come from, and why.

"Sharon is one of the partners in the land Stop N Shop wants to buy." Nicole didn't get to finish. Tom eagerly added his contribution.

"She also manages the investment group, and is the broker representing both parties in the sale." He gave a "so there" nod toward Ray.

"You're making a big thing out of nothing," Ray said, disgust obvious in both voice and face. "The important thing is to get the deal done, not how you do it. And don't forget, Hank had a financial interest in that store. He was one of the partners, too, and was a cinch to get the contract to build the store. That didn't stop him from voting."

"Yes, it did." Dottie's voice was firmer than I'd ever heard it. "Hank was going to abstain, he told me so. He was trying to get some of the undecided people to be sensible, but he wasn't going to vote. Hank was an honorable man."

That wasn't the way I'd heard it, but maybe Hank had separate standards for personal behavior and business. I took another look at Dottie. She stared defiantly at Ray, her mouth set, her hands clenched. Perhaps Aunt Mary and Pat Bennington had something. Dottie's expression suggested her defense of Hank was something more than standing up for an "honorable man."

"Wouldn't it be nice if some other people around here had that reputation," Tom muttered. Nicole glanced up at him, then, a little nervously, back at Ray.

"Now, listen here," Ray began, belligerence ripe in his voice, "if you're calling me unethical, or saying I'm not honorable, you better have proof. Good proof."

He moved toward Tom, who stood his ground.

Dottie gave a little moan.

Nicole, a nervous laugh. "He never mentioned your name, Ray. Don't be so touchy."

Tom didn't help matters. "If the shoe fits."

"Now, listen here." This time Ray raised his clenched fist.

"Hank didn't think you were so darn ethical." Tom clenched his own. "He said he'd have your license taken away. Could he have, Ray? Did that make you so upset you hit him over the head with a brick?"

"Hey, you can't get away with accusing me of murder. Hank didn't have one shred of proof I ever did anything wrong." Ray's scowl turned into a sneer. "Besides, if we're talking about murder, how about you? It was your little wife Hank was trying to hit on. Made you pretty mad, didn't it, Tommy?"

I watched Tom's face flush with rage. His glasses slipped down his nose, but instead of pushing them up again he pulled back his right arm and started toward Ray. I was sure he was going to let fly and we would be treated to an old-fashioned fistfight. *Should I do something? What?* One more thing real estate school hadn't prepared me for.

The door opened. I could hear it, but my back was turned and I couldn't see who it was. I could guess, though. Tom's hand dropped to his side and his face turned to chalk. Ray's jutting chin dropped and an ingratiating smile started to form. Nicole still looked scared, Dottie looked relieved. Dan had arrived.

"Hi," was all he said. It had more effect than if he'd yelled through a bullhorn to clear the room.

"Ah, Dan." Ray tried hard to smile. "Good to see you. Ah…"

"Good to see you, too, Ray." Dan's voice was mild. Deliberately mild. I could have told Ray that was a dangerous sign, but didn't. Instead, I turned toward him and smiled. I got one back before he turned to the rest of the group. "What's going on? You all look a little agitated."

"Nothing, nothing," Ray said hurriedly. "We were, ah, talking about poor Hank. Such a tragedy."

It was almost funny watching Ray try to look pious.

"Are you making any progress finding out who did it?" Dottie's voice was soft, and somehow sad.

"We're working on it. Don't worry. This is one murderer who won't get away."

"Oh? How can you be so sure?" Ray's question was innocent, but he let the doubt in his voice show through.

Dan heard it. His expression didn't change as he looked at him. He didn't say a word until Ray started to squirm. "Through painstaking investigation, Ray. That's how we solve all our cases."

Ray flushed, at least he had that much sense, but he couldn't quite put his needle away. "And who are you going to investigate?" He looked pointedly at Tom.

"You, Ray." I thought Ray was going to faint. "We have some questions to ask you, and I'm sure you'll be only too glad to answer them. Won't you?"

Ray gulped and nodded.

For the first time Dan turned toward Tom and Nicole, who seemed to be trying to fade into the background. "We'll need to ask you some questions, too. And you, Dottie."

"What kind of questions?" She seemed the only one of the three capable of speech.

"When you saw Hank last, what he said, that kind of thing. I'll also need your fingerprints. None of you mind, do you?"

"Fingerprints?" Tom said faintly.

"Yes. That's all right, isn't it?" There was an edge to Dan's voice that said it had better be.

"Sure, sure. I just wondered why?"

"That house is full of fingerprints. Workmen, mostly, but all of you went out to look at it a couple of days ago. Right?"

Ray, Nicole and Tom all looked at each other. Nicole nodded.

"If your prints come up, we can use them for elimination."

"Elimination?" Nicole sounded a little hopeful.

"Uh-huh," Dan replied. "Then I can count on all of you? Good. Give the station a call. They'll set up appointments for you. Now, Ellie." He turned to me. "It's your turn. You won't mind a little ink on your fingers, will you?"

"Not a bit." I made my voice determinedly cheerful. "I can hardly wait."

Dan held the office door open for me, and we sailed out.

"You didn't need to spread it on quite that thick." I could barely hear him as the door closed behind us.

"Yeah? It sure sounded like someone needed to. What's the matter with all of them?"

"I don't know, but it's going to be interesting to find out."

NINE

DAN STARTED OFF down the sidewalk, me beside him.

"Where's your car?"

He stopped, looked down at me with a grin. "Oh, Ellie. You lived in Los Angeles too long. This is Santa Louisa. Here, we walk."

Our office was downtown, directly across from a picture-book park, complete with a fountain, bandstand and a much-loved original old brick Carnegie library, overflowing with books. Ours was the kind of town that invited walking, browsing, stopping and chatting. I'd almost forgotten.

Dan and I started down one of the brick paths that wandered through the park. Across the street, I could see the old Inn clearly through the leafless trees where it sat in majestic splendor. It was a landmark in its own right. There'd been a rumor going around for years that Jesse James stayed there and that he had a secret tunnel made for a quick escape, but no one had been able to prove it. All of the guest rooms opened out onto the gardens complete with fishpond and water lilies.

It was the most popular place in town for wedding receptions, and half our brides had pictures of themselves wandering romantically with their grooms under the ancient oaks. Lots of things had changed in the twenty or more years I had been gone, but not this. I was momentarily transported back to childhood, with all the feeling of peace and security that went with that time. Unfortunately that didn't last. We had reached the small police station.

A plump, motherly-type woman was sitting behind the counter, looking all wrong in her blue uniform. She belonged at one of Aunt Mary's church sales, or leading a Girl Scout troop, anywhere but here.

She bustled around from behind the counter, giving us both a toothy smile. "You the one needs her fingerprints taken? Come right over here, dear. Won't take but a minute, then you can go in that other room and Sergeant Riker can take your statement. Don't you worry none, dear. None of us bite. Do we, Chief?"

She laughed heartily. I heard Dan chuckle.

"Take good care of her, Hazel. And wash her hands off good. I'm taking her to lunch later and I'd like her presentable."

Hazel gave me a second look. "He's taking you to lunch? Well, don't that beat all." She looked me up and down again, and nodded. I must have passed because she grinned, grabbed me by the hand and practically pulled me behind the counter. Dan disappeared through a door marked, appropriately, Chief of Police, and my thumb was already rolling in ink.

Sergeant Riker was the thin policeman from yesterday with the "Joe Friday" voice. Evidently I hadn't made a good impression on him for he ignored my attempt to be friendly, skipped the formalities, and went right to the questions.

"Why were you at the house at four o'clock on a Sunday afternoon? Why did you go upstairs? Did you touch anything?"

I'd tried to answer factually and unemotionally, but now I blurted out, "Like what?"

"Well—" Riker lost his detached attitude and looked a little flustered "—like the closet door, or…"

"Are you trying to ask me if I touched the body?" I asked, incredulous.

"Well…" Riker paused before he took the plunge. "Yes. Did you?"

Hank, lying in that closet, appeared before me and I shuddered. "No," I said. If he wanted more, he was going to have to ask. He didn't.

Finally, we were through. Riker presented me with a copy of my statement. I read it, signed, and walked back out to the tiny reception room. Hazel sat on a stool, reading a book. She hastily pulled it into her lap, but not before I caught a glimpse of the cover. A hero with bared chest, a heroine with heaving bosoms. Maybe I needed to rethink the Girl Scout part.

I knocked on the closed door of Dan's office, heard a muffled "come in," so I did. Dan was on the phone. He waved me to one of the two chairs in front of his desk while he continued to scribble notes on a legal pad. I thought only lawyers and real estate agents used them. Maybe not.

The chairs were 1960s-modern and covered in brown vinyl. I chose the one without a crack in the seat and looked around. A reasonably good-size room but crammed with stuff. Open shelves on one wall overflowed with manuals, boxes, folders, a computer terminal, fax machine and a radio of some kind making soft static noises. The opposite wall was filled with file cabinets, more files piled on top of them. The wall behind Dan held a window, one that looked out on the back side of the park, and on his desk, in a silver frame, was a picture of a pretty young woman with long black hair and deep brown eyes holding a boy about three. The boy was a darker version of his father.

Dan saw me look at the picture, and his eyes

lingered on it also. He didn't say anything, however, only hung up the phone and smiled at me.

"All done?" He glanced down at my hands. I stuck my tongue out at him and he laughed. "Come on," he said. "Let's go eat."

Hazel looked up from her book as we passed through. "Have fun." That devilish grin must have come from something she read in the book she kept trying to hide. It couldn't have been meant for us.

TEN

DAN STEERED ME away from the park, down past the old clock tower.

"Where are we going?"

"To the Yum Yum."

"Oh, no." I stopped in my tracks. "Not that place."

"Why not?" Dan looked down at me, startled. "Don't you like it?"

"I've never been there, but I've been by it. It reeks 'cute.' All those wooden ducks with bows, plastic plants and gingham curtains. I'll bet there's nothing on the menu but herbal tea and anemic sandwiches with adorable names."

Dan started to laugh. "Are you in for a surprise. Come on." He grabbed my hand and pulled me through the door.

The smell when we entered was one step this side of heaven. We edged our way between crowded tables to the only empty one, way in the back. There was nothing anemic about the portions on the plates in front of the people we passed. Dan was obviously a regular, for the waitress, a small, wiry type with overly permed blond hair and an energetic manner, came loping over to greet us before we were all the way seated.

"Soup's tomato bisque, muffins are corn bread or pumpkin. Special's meatloaf with mashed potatoes. You havin' that?"

Dan sighed. "Just soup, Ruthie. Corn bread muffins."

"You havin' the same?" she asked me, filling both our coffee cups. "Say, you're Ellen McKenzie, aren't you? The one who found Hank in that house. Terrible thing, just terrible. Be right back with your soup."

She rushed off without bothering for an answer.

"I think you'll like the soup." Dan's voice was mild, a smile hiding behind his mustache.

"Humm." I looked around. "I hope so. It didn't seem I had much choice. How did she know who I am?"

"Small town," was the cryptic reply.

"I know it's a small town," I said a little tartly. "I grew up here, remember?"

"I remember."

I looked at him for a second, started to say something. I decided to stick to the present. "Dan, listen." I leaned over the table toward him, away from the loud hum of conversation. "When you came in the office, Tom and Ray were fighting."

"I saw that."

"Well, what you didn't see, or hear, was they

were accusing each other of Hank's murder. You don't think either of them could have done it, do you?"

Instead of an answer, I got a question. "Why does Ray think Tom might have killed Hank?"

"Oh," I said, feeling I'd let the cat out of the bag. Dan knew about the controversy between Hank and Ray, but he evidently didn't know about Tom and Hank's argument, and I didn't want to be the one to tell him.

"Well?" He watched me expectantly. I didn't have a choice, so I took a deep breath and started, but only got out one word.

"Here we are," Ruthie sang. She set down huge bowls of soup giving off clouds of mouthwatering aroma, an overflowing basket of fresh, warm muffins, a dish of wrapped butter squares, and filled the coffee cups again. She pushed the cream toward Dan and paused, half-filled coffeepot in one hand.

"You gettin' anywhere findin' out who killed Hank?"

"Now, Ruthie." Dan picked up his spoon. "It's early days. We'll find him."

"You better," she said crisply. "Hank was a good man." She waved the coffeepot in the air. I ducked. She gave me a surprised look and trotted off.

"She never spills it."

"There's always a first time." I reached for a muffin and buttered it, hoping Dan had forgotten I was to tell him about Tom.

"Go on, Ellie. Why would Tom Chambers want to kill Hank Sawyer?"

I was trapped.

"Hank made a pass at Nicole and Tom told him to lay off." I took a large mouthful of soup. Big mistake. It was still boiling. I grabbed for the water glass, swallowed quickly and accepted the napkin Dan handed me to wipe my watery eyes.

"My, my. Sharon told me Hank had started in on Nicole, but I didn't realize— You all right? Need another napkin?"

I shook my head and very gingerly took a sip of soup.

"So—" Dan's spoon hovered halfway between his bowl and his mouth "—knowing Tom's temper, he probably made quite a production out of telling Hank to lay off. And, knowing Hank, he probably ignored Tom. Or laughed. Right?"

"I don't know. Sharon told me. I never saw any of it. I only met Hank once, last Saturday when he came in the office, looking for Sharon."

Dan sighed. "Hank was really pretty harmless, but he somehow felt obligated to try. I'm sure your turn would have come. You're pretty. And shapely."

Dan was looking down at his soup, so he didn't see my flush. How lucky I'd worn my new dress. It was kind to my waistline. And it was nice to get a compliment, even if it was an offhand one. Brian hadn't given me one in years. But that brought another thought. Compliments. Dottie. Hank. No, that wasn't possible.

"What?" Dan said. "You're thinking something. What is it?"

"How do you know? You're not a mind reader."

"I don't have to be. I can read your face. I always could."

"That's not true," I replied with great dignity. "I'm not thinking anything."

"It is too true, and you might as well tell me." He sipped his soup.

I put down my soupspoon and stared into the bowl. I was torn between not wanting to drag Dottie into this and the need to hear Dan say how silly it was to even think she could be implicated. "It's really nothing. But what you said about Hank, and making passes… I was over at Aunt Mary's and…"

"You sure are dragging this out." Dan looked more curious by the minute. He finished his soup and started on his second muffin.

And I'm just deeding that curiosity, I thought. "Pat Bennington was there. Do you know her?"

Dan nodded. "I play poker with her husband, Carl. He's a veterinarian."

"Well, Pat said Hank had been seeing a lot of Dottie Fielding lately. You know, Dottie, our office secretary. They all belong to that amateur theater group and…"

I broke off. Dan's muffin hadn't quite made it to his mouth, a good thing, because he exploded laughing. "Hank and Dottie Fielding? You've got to be kidding."

"I'm not. Besides, why not Dottie?"

Dan didn't bother to answer. We both knew.

"Hank was really paying attention to Dottie?"

"Even took her home one night last week." I nodded to emphasize my point.

"Pat and Mary think Dottie might have mistaken Hank's attention for something more than a casual…"

"I'm sure they're wrong." I started to feel a little anxious. He wasn't supposed to take this seriously.

"It doesn't seem likely, but then, it's been known to happen."

"That's what Aunt Mary said." I didn't like the thoughtful look on Dan's face. He needed distracting. "There was some other excitement at the office today."

"Oh? What?" he asked, but he didn't look as if he was paying much attention.

"Evidently Benjamin Lockwood came storming in, yelling he was going to take Hank's place on the Planning Commission and make sure the Stop N Shop store won't come and that Sharon couldn't stop him."

Now I had his attention.

"Benjamin." He frowned, a sort of concerned, worried frown. "He gets more crazy every day. Have you been in the Emporium since you've been back?"

I shook my head.

"Benjamin's changed it all around. The way he goes on, you'd think it was better than, what's that big store all you women like?"

"Nordstrom."

"That's it. He's been having a fit ever since he heard about Stop N Shop, and he's got a lot of support, especially from the other downtown merchants."

"Why? This town is growing. I couldn't believe it when I came home. Why, we even have a new supermarket."

"Yeah, and the local market has fewer customers. No, the merchants have a right to be worried, but if Stop N Shop doesn't come, some other store will, if not this year, then next. The locals have to look at what they're doing and learn to do it better, or different, because you can't stop change."

"Does that mean you think Benjamin might have killed Hank? To somehow keep the new store from coming?" I was amazed, first that he could suspect an old man, and second, that he thought something as simple as a new store could be a motive.

"I don't know who killed him, or why." For the first time there was no smile under that neat little mustache, no laugh lines around his eyes. "But the Emporium is everything to Benjamin, and Stop N Shop will put him out of business. He's not so crazy he doesn't know that. He also knew Hank wanted that store, and was doing some heavy lobbying to make sure it got built."

I put my coffee cup down with a clink. "Good grief, Dan. It sounds like half the people in this town had some kind of reason to eliminate Hank Sawyer. The only person we've left out is his wife, Vera."

"We haven't left her out. Are you ready to go?"

"Oh." I remembered my conversation with Aunt Mary and couldn't help thinking what a tidy solution Vera made. Probably too tidy.

I opened my purse, but Dan already had money on the table and his chair pushed back.

"Thanks," I said. I almost said I'd get the check next time, but caught myself. Would there be a next time?

"You can make me dinner some night." That little smile was back.

The man had read my face again.

ELEVEN

Dan left me at the library to go back to the station. I continued on to the office with some reluctance. I barely knew any of these people and felt, somehow, I had been thrust into the middle of their personal lives. It was none of my business if Dottie had, in her middle age, finally managed to have an affair, if Tom was jealous of his wife, if Ray skirted the fine edges of ethical behavior. Unless, of course, one of them was a murderer.

I shuddered, thought of Benjamin, rejected the idea, and decided the murderer was either Vera or some stranger.

Tom was in the conference room with clients, Dottie was engrossed in doing something on her computer and the rest of the office was empty.

"Ellen, you have a message." Dottie didn't look up.

"Me? A message?" I headed for my desk. Maybe Bernice had changed her mind, and she and Harvey wanted to buy the house after all.

Call Alice Ives, the message said. Who was Alice Ives? The name sounded familiar but— Of course. Alice. One of my mother's bridge friends. We'd called them the "faithful four" because they never missed a Tuesday afternoon. Did women do that anymore? I wondered as I dialed her number.

"Ellen, dear, how lovely to hear your voice, and how is your dear mother and all your lovely family?"

I sighed and made all the appropriate noises. I had forgotten how Alice prattled on, filling conversation with hurried, breathless little phrases that meant nothing. Unfortunately, you had to pay attention or you'd miss the important bits. I almost did.

"And that's why I want you to list my house, because I really think Florida would be closer to the children and…"

List her house? I couldn't believe it.

"Alice," I interrupted, "I'd love to. When would you like me to come over?"

"Well, dear, I always say, if you are going to do something, don't put it off. Just get right in and do it, and I've made up my mind, so I think we should get started, but not today. This week though. Let's see, tomorrow is my hair appointment, Wednesday is poor Hank's funeral—I must call Vera—and Thursday is something, I just can't remember, but I know there is something—maybe Friday?

Why don't you call me on Thursday. We'll set up a time then. Is that all right?"

I hung up with mixed feelings. My first listing! That was exciting. But Alice Ives, how was I going to handle Alice? She meant well, but it was almost impossible to keep her on track. And her house! How did you go about pricing a house like her lovely, large, well-kept, but aging giant? It was on a double lot, with lots of trees, but I'd be willing to bet the plumbing hadn't been upgraded since the thirties. I was going to need some help on this one.

Dottie came over to my desk and handed me the message book. "I'm going home to lunch. I'll be back in about an hour. Nicole is out showing property, so is Ray, and Sharon is still working on the Planning Commission emergency."

I looked up, studying her, wondering if her face would give some sign of how she felt. Remorse? Grief? Luckily, Dottie took my silence for nervousness at being left alone.

"If you get a question you can't handle, buzz Tom in the conference room. You'll be fine, Ellen. Really."

I watched her carefully cover her computer, replace her pencils in a red, white and blue striped mug, square up all the files she had been working on, then work herself into a heavy dark brown sweater and leave. She gave me her usual timid smile as she went out the door.

I spent the rest of the afternoon answering the phone, which got easier, and trying to figure out what to do about Alice's house, which didn't. Tom finished with his clients, then paused by my desk and made a few non-committal comments while waiting for Nicole. She came in, said something to him in a low tone, and they both left. Ray breezed in, gave Dottie, who was back from lunch, a raft of instructions, then made a point of talking loudly on the phone. I wasn't impressed.

It was five-thirty when Sharon finally came back. Dottie had once more tidied her desk and had gone. I was putting the phones on answering service and was also ready to leave.

"You look exhausted." I paused, curious. "What happened?"

"We fought. All afternoon. But Benjamin isn't going to get Hank's seat. Evan Hopkins is. He owns an antiques store, so he's not afraid Stop N Shop will put him out of business. Now we'll wait and see what happens."

"Do you think Stop N Shop really might not come?"

"They'd better come. I've worked on this too long and too hard to have it crash now." Her voice was grim and in spite of how tired she looked, the set of her jaw said determination. "This town needs it. The only place we have to shop is the Emporium, and that's plain pathetic."

I took in Sharon's long, flowered silk skirt, her matching silk sweater, low-heeled Italian pumps and delicate gold chain. It was obvious she didn't shop at the Emporium, but I didn't think she'd be doing too much at a discount store like Stop N Shop either.

"I hear Dan Dunham took you to lunch." She smiled at me. "Renewing old friendships?"

I could feel my face get stiff. How did she know? "Something like that."

"I remember how you used to tag after Dan when you were little. You had quite a crush on him."

"He lived next door. I thought of him as a brother. I still do."

"Of course." Sharon dismissed the subject as of only passing interest. "I'll collect my messages and head for home. See you in the morning."

I took my cue and left. Sharon's intimation that Dan taking me to lunch might mean something made me uncomfortable. Hazel had intimated much the same thing. I couldn't possibly think of Dan in any way but as a friend, and I was sure that was how he thought of me. Wasn't it? Of course it was.

It seemed I was on the phone all evening. First my parents called from Scottsdale. They had heard about Hank. I was no longer surprised. Of course the long arm of the Santa Louisa information network had reached them.

"Are you all right?" That was my father.

"I hear you and Dan Dunham had lunch." Mother had a knack of getting to the important things.

"How's your golf game coming?" I asked them both.

Later, Aunt Mary called. "How was lunch?"

"You mean you don't know?"

"Don't get smart," I was told. "I went over to see Vera. She's really in a bad way. Her oldest daughter's here from New Jersey, and it's a good thing. Vera's not coping well. Couldn't make any decisions about the funeral, the casket or anything. It was a good thing the church committee was there to take charge."

I agreed it was indeed a good thing, then, a little slowly because I didn't want to seem like a ghoul, asked, "So you don't think Vera was the one?"

"The one what?" Aunt Mary asked. "Oh. To kill Hank? I never did. That was your theory."

"I guess it was, but it sure tied things up neatly."

"Tying things up is something you don't have to worry about. Leave that to Dan. That reminds me, why don't you two come to dinner Wednesday night?"

"I'd love to, but I can't answer for him. Have you called him?"

"I thought I'd leave that up to you," she purred. "Let me know."

"What's the matter with all these people?" I asked Jake as I hung up. "They're practically throwing Dan at me. Or me at him."

The cat sat on the table and looked at me without answering.

"And another thing. I wasn't trying to set Vera up as a murderer, or anybody else. But I found the body—I work with half the suspects. That doesn't make me curious, does it? It makes me involved." I stared at the cat, waiting for an answer. He yawned.

TWELVE

THE SUN STREAMED in my bedroom window with the tiniest hint of warmth, and there were just enough clouds left over to make the morning interesting. I watched them float slowly by as I sipped my morning coffee, wondering if the day was going to be interesting as well.

I had nothing scheduled at the office, and after yesterday, wasn't eager to make an appearance. There were still boxes unpacked in my dining room, a task I felt more equal to than real estate, so I concentrated on stacking china plates in the hutch. Brian, suffering from an unexpected attack of guilt, had let me take most of the things I had grown attached to over the years, and I had come away with more than my parents' old house could hold. Now I had to figure out what to do with some of it.

By the time I had hung a few more pictures, repacked several boxes, stored them in the workshop next to the garage and put the empty ones out for the trash man, it was after ten. I was out of excuses, so I exchanged jeans and sweatshirt for wool slacks and a sweater and headed for the office.

Sharon looked up as I came in and followed me over to my desk.

"I understand you are going to list Alice Ives's old house."

I nodded, too surprised to say anything. How did everyone know all this stuff?

"Have you talked to her about a market price?"

"No," I admitted. "I have no idea how to go about it."

"You might start by going to look at these." She put several sheets of paper down on my desk. "These are listings of homes a little like Alice's. They'll be good comparables." She walked away.

I can take a hint. I picked up the phone, made an appointment to see each house on the sheets and left.

I'll bet Sharon wouldn't let a little thing like unpacking dishes deter her from working real estate, I thought. She seemed to be doing something constantly. Not that the others didn't work hard. Everyone was either on the phone or running out the door to an appointment. Once I got the hang of this, it looked like my free time would be gone. I shrugged as I climbed in my car. Sounded good to me.

This is the part of real estate I'm going to like

best, I thought as I pulled up to the first house. The three I had scheduled had all been built during different periods. This one dated back to the late eighteen hundreds. The high ceilings, richly ornate moldings and long, narrow rooms, one opening on to another, transported me back to another time. The people who owned the home had done a marvelous job restoring it. Patterned carpets, cabbage roses on the wallpaper, even the old chandeliers still hung from the ten-foot ceilings. The bathrooms had claw-foot tubs with lace shower curtains on round rods above them, but I was amused to note the kitchen stove burned gas, not wood. I stood for a moment, looking at the steep stairs leading up to the bedrooms and down into the basement, and marveled at those women, trailing skirts and petticoats, traveling those treacherous steps many times a day.

The next two places were closer in age and style to Alice's, built just after the turn of the century. Larger rooms, wider stairs, much better kitchens, but still no closet space. Neither of them was kept as well as Aunt Mary's or mine. I wondered what I would find at Alice's.

By now I was hungry, so I stopped at Kenny's market for some lunch. My mother had always shopped there, and my mouth watered at the thought of homemade breads, mile-high sandwiches and Mrs. Kenny's lemon pie. The deli counter had given way to prepackaged meats, the fresh-bread smell had disappeared behind plastic wrap and the only pie was in the freezer. I had to content myself with something on a foam tray and a carton of milk.

Sighing, I returned to the office to munch my greasy tuna and work on my presentation for Alice, but my mind kept drifting away from real estate and onto other matters.

Finally, I grabbed the telephone book, wrote down two addresses, gathered my things together and said to Dottie, "If anyone needs me, I can be reached at home later."

"All right." She looked up at me intently. "Ellen…"

I stopped expectantly and waited.

"Oh, nothing." She dropped her eyes to the desk again and her voice died away.

I hesitated, not wanting to walk out on her. "I'm in no hurry. If there's something I can do…?"

"No, it's just that…"

She broke off as Ray appeared at her desk and dropped a couple of files on top of her other work. "Here's two more listings." He puffed out his chest a little. "Two in one day, not bad. We need to get these in the computer right away."

Dottie ducked her head and said nothing. Ray turned toward me.

"It won't be long, Ellen, and you'll be doing a lot of business, too. Maybe not as much as I do, but a lot."

Now there was a man who knew how to give a compliment.

"You got an appointment?" he went on, striding toward the door, holding it open for me. I glanced back at Dottie, who had her eyes glued onto her desk. Oh, well.

"You might say that," I told Ray, and, head held high, walked out the door.

THIRTEEN

I DROVE SLOWLY up in front of the Sawyers' house and parked. *This isn't a good idea,* I told myself. However, my father used to play golf with Hank, my aunt was on the church committee with Vera, it was my duty to pay a condolence call. Wasn't it?

I stared at the house for a moment, trying to decide. The house surprised me. Hank was supposed to be the most successful builder in town, and I had expected a home that would show off his skills, also his financial condition. This house was nice enough, but hardly prestigious. A rambling ranch style with the shake roof and diamond-pattern windows popular years ago, it showed a lot of loving care in its neatly mowed lawn and trimmed bushes. Still, it spoke gently of middle age. A few winter pansies poked their heads out of wine barrels on the front porch, and the camellias and azaleas banked against the front of the house looked as if they were trying to beat spring and bloom early.

There were several cars parked in the driveway and in front of the house. As I watched, the front door opened. A woman came down the front steps and another, younger one said, "Thank you again." She paused, looked at me sitting in the car, then slowly went back inside and closed the door.

No more decisions. I'd been spotted, and it would be the ultimate insult to the bereaved if I didn't go inside. Too bad I didn't have an offering. I'd forgotten the small-town custom about funerals. You take two things to the family, sympathy and food. By now the Sawyer kitchen would be filled with more hams, platters of fried chicken, casseroles, Jell-O salads and chocolate cakes than the family would be able to eat in a month. However, since the entire town would be stopping by tomorrow after the service, leftovers wouldn't be a problem.

I rang the bell and the same young woman answered. She was in her early twenties and probably usually very pretty. Now she looked drawn and tired, her long, dark hair pulled back carelessly and fastened with a large barrette.

"Yes?" She looked at me uncertainly, not sure if she should know me.

"I'm Ellen McKenzie. I stopped by to see Mrs. Sawyer and offer my condolences." I was feeling more uncomfortable by the minute. Why on earth had I thought this a good idea? "This is probably a bad time. If you would tell her I stopped by and how sorry I am, I'd be grateful."

I started to back away from the door in preparation for a cowardly flight back to my car.

"Oh, no." She opened the door wide. "I'm sure Gran would want to see you. Please come in."

Escape now impossible, I stepped into the small entryway. I could hear the low murmur of voices coming from what was plainly the kitchen. A woman about my age came through the door into the entry hall where we were standing.

"Ellen Page, how good of you to come. Only it's McKenzie now, isn't it. I'm Violet. You probably don't remember me. I was a senior when you were a freshman. Come into the living room, please. Mother's in there."

She was right. I didn't remember her, and I felt more and more that coming was a mistake.

I'm not sure I had a mental picture of Vera, but if I had, it wasn't this small, slightly plump woman sitting in the overstuffed rocker, her feet barely touching the floor. Her salt-and-pepper hair looked as if it had been smartly styled a few days ago, but hardly combed today. The room was quite warm, but she had the cardigan sweater she wore pulled tightly around her. Eyes red rimmed, face gray, she seemed consumed with grief and shock. She looked up when we came in, but I thought she was only partly conscious of our presence.

"Mother, Ellen McKenzie has come to see you. You remember her, don't you? She's a Page." The daughter turned to me with a sad try of a smile. "Will you excuse me? I have to get back to the kitchen. Thank you again for coming."

I stood for a moment, at a complete loss for words. Every ounce of my being wanted to turn and run. Suddenly, Vera looked up at me and said, "Sit down, Ellen. It was thoughtful of you to come. I remember your parents, of course. I heard they moved away somewhere."

I murmured, "Yes, Scottsdale. The weather, you know." It was obvious Vera wasn't interested in where my parents had gone, or why.

"Dan told us you found my husband," she went on, her tone flat. "I'm so sorry. It must have been horrible for you." Then she broke off, her whole body appeared to shudder, and she was still again.

Not as horrible as this, I thought, while I heard myself say, "I'm so sorry, Mrs. Sawyer. Such a terrible thing. My parents send their deepest sympathy."

"Thank them for me. Your father and Hank used to…" She took a deep breath and seemed to stare off into space.

"If it's any consolation," I said, wondering how

soon I could escape, "everyone I talk with says what a good man Hank was, fun to be with, a good friend."

"And a wonderful, loving husband and father." She said this almost defensively, looking at a picture of a tall, handsome blond man standing with his arm around the young girl who had opened the front door for me. She was in graduation cap and gown and both were smiling at the camera. It was easy to see how Hank made so many conquests. He looked much younger than Vera, and his charm and good humor almost leapt out of the frame. My expression must have given away my thoughts because for the first time I seemed to have her full attention.

"He was, you know. A good husband. Oh, I know what people said. They've been saying it for years. But it wasn't true." Her eyes blazed and her voice was a harsh whisper. "He flirted a little, that was all. He liked to laugh, to joke, but it was me he loved. I used to tell him, you've got to be careful. People will talk. He'd say, 'Let 'em. You know I love you, don't you, Vera.' I did know. He loved me."

Her voice faded. "And now he's gone. Gone. Just like that..." She sat back in her chair, leaving me and the room we were in behind.

This was not fun, I decided. Books made everything seem so easy, but watching Vera was agonizing. I wanted to ask her a question and now, before I lost my nerve, I blurted it out. "Was Hank planning to meet someone Sunday afternoon? At the new house he was building?"

"I don't know." I could barely hear her words. It was plain I no longer existed.

I got up, murmured vague words, and started into the hallway. The daughter, Violet, appeared.

"It was really nice of you to take the time to come, Ellen. Mother's in a bad way, and we still have to get through tomorrow." She paused, reached into her apron pocket for a tissue and daubed at her eyes before continuing. "My sister and I've been talking. We think it best if I take Mother home with me for a while. We've got some decisions to make, but none of us are thinking straight right now." She swallowed hard. "You work with Sharon Harper, don't you? Would you tell her I'll call her in a week or so about Dad's properties? I'd appreciate it, Ellen, and thanks again for coming." She stuck out her hand; I placed mine in it, and quickly made my escape, my head and emotions in a whirl.

I climbed into my car, trying to sort out my thoughts. Vera Sawyer didn't look or act like a murderer; her grief and shock were too genuine. *Those poor people,* I thought as I started the car, *what a terrible thing to go through.* But an unwilling idea crept into my mind. Vera couldn't really have gone along all those years and believed him. Could she? She was pretty fierce about insisting Hank loved only her. Suppose, somehow, she had been forced to see the truth? Could she have confronted him Sunday afternoon, in that empty house? Finally lost her temper, thrown a brick at him, then, in a fit of desperation as he was lying there, dragged him— No, it didn't seem possible. Still...

By this time I was back in town, passing the once familiar Emporium. Impulsively, I swung the wheel hard and pulled into one of the many empty parking spaces in front of it. Everyone kept talking about the Emporium and Benjamin. It was time I saw for myself.

Years ago the Emporium and J. C. Penney were the only places in town to shop. If they didn't have it, you went without. The Emporium had some of everything. Clothes for all ages, housewares, hardware, even halters, lead ropes, calf-nursing bottles and, of course, rifles and ammunition. It also had one of those wonderful tube systems where the clerk put your money and sales slip in a round cylinder, pulled the rope and, like magic, it flew up a cable to ladies sitting on a mezzanine, looking down on the lesser mortals below. They leisurely checked everything, put the change back into the tube and—zip—back it came. Growing up, I thought that flying tube the most exciting thing I had ever seen, and the Emporium the most magnificent store anywhere.

I walked in, prepared for changes, but nevertheless looking for my magic tube and the ladies who sat serenely above us all. Instead, I found a tired old building, all its natural charm and dignity covered over with cheap plastic and artificial glitz. No more housewares, no more hardware, only a few racks of bad, discount-quality clothes, at what appeared to be inflated prices. Hank had been right. Stop N Shop wouldn't drive Benjamin out of business. He was doing just fine all by himself.

I wandered around, picking things up, putting them down, thinking someone would appear and offer to help me. Then I could ask for Benjamin. No one did. I kept sorting through the scanty selection, finally ending up with a package of socks in my hand.

"—help you," someone said from behind my back.

I whirled around to find a wispy little old lady looking at me disapprovingly through too-large glasses.

"Ah," I said, feeling as guilty as though I had been caught stealing. "Do you have these in blue?"

"No," she said, and walked off.

Shopping at the Emporium was a real challenge.

"Well, well, well, look who's here. It's little Ellen Page. Heard you'd come home."

There was Benjamin, coming down the aisle toward me, thrusting his long, bony face toward mine. Amazing how little he'd changed. A little less hair, more sprinkles of gray, but still the same tall, stringy man with slightly stooped shoulders, the same prominent Adam's apple and the same pale eyes. If I hadn't known better, I'd have sworn he even had on the same clothes. Slightly baggy wash pants, plaid shirt open at the throat, an over-large green cardigan sweater, never buttoned, that always seemed to be trying to catch up to him.

"Whadda you think of our new look, Ellen?" He made a great swoop of his arm, taking in the whole store. "Not the same store you knew as a kid, huh?" He looked around with pride. "Surprised?"

"Oh, yes." I could say that with all honesty. "Very surprised. My, it's been a long time. How have you been?"

"Just so-so, Ellen," he said, answering me literally. "Suppose you heard that Rose died. Been almost three years now." He seemed a little lost, shook himself slightly and went on. "It was after that I did the store over. Needed something to distract me." He forced a smile. "Hasn't helped business, though. This town isn't what it used to be. All the old families, like your folks, leavin'. New ones comin', but they got no loyalty. All they do is complain."

Yes, I thought as I looked around the store again, I could believe that.

"I don't know about folks anymore," he went on. "Used to be, people'd be satisfied. Now, they keep goin' on about bigger, better, more, want everythin' new."

"New," I repeated. "You mean like the new store that's coming, Stop N Shop?"

"We'll see what's comin' and what's not." Benjamin actually hissed. I could see spittle fly out of his mouth. I stepped back. He didn't seem to notice. "That crowd at City Hall, talkin' about how it'd be good for the town. Balderdash! It'd put all us downtown people out of business, that's what."

"Oh, well." I took another step back and made my voice as noncommittal as I could. "Maybe not."

"Why, they want me to go to some fool class to learn to compete." Benjamin ignored my weak comment. "Me! I've run this store for forty years, and my father before me. Don't need no city boys telling me how to do it. It's them new people trying to push this through, but I still got a trick or two up my sleeve. They're in for a fight, let me tell you."

Benjamin was getting more and more agitated, an angry flush working its way up his pasty white face. It was scary watching him. I tried to think of something to calm him down, but instead I blurted out, "Is that why you wanted Hank's seat on the Planning Commission?"

The flush deepened. He's going to have a stroke, I thought, and it's all my fault. But Benjamin took a deep breath, the red turned to pink and a sorrowful expression replaced his angry one.

"Hank Sawyer was one of my best friends in the world," he said. "I'm goin' to be one of the pall bearers tomorrow, but I'll never forget how he turned on us downtown people. He was a clear thinkin' man on most things, but on this, I just couldn't get him to see reason. It was greed. Pure and simple. Greed."

"Greed? What do you mean?"

"Hank stood to make a bundle if that store came. Said he wouldn't vote, but folks knew how he stood, and Hank had a lot of influence in this town. He woulda got his store. Now, we'll see. You gonna pay me for those socks, Ellen?"

I gaped at Benjamin, handed him some money, took my package and my change and fled.

FOURTEEN

I SAT IN THE CAR, engine idling, trying to absorb what I had heard. Benjamin hadn't admitted to murder, but he'd given himself a great motive. A better one than Tom's, a better one than Ray's and way better than Dottie's. Benjamin would benefit with Hank dead, or he thought he would, and he'd already gone after Hank once with a hammer. The thought made me queasy. Benjamin had given me lollipops when I was little; he'd talked my mother into letting me have high heels, sort of, for junior-high graduation. He couldn't be a cold-blooded killer. He just couldn't!

I found myself staring at a shop a couple of doors down from the Emporium. There was something familiar about it, but what? Of course, it was Mom and Pop's Ice Cream Store. The best hot fudge sundaes anywhere, real strawberry sodas and homemade berry pie with vanilla ice cream. We used to walk down here with my parents on hot summer nights and bring home wonderful treats that we'd eat sitting on the steps of our front porch. Only this sign didn't say Mom and Pop's. It said Skinny Haven, Nonfat Frozen Yogurt.

Wouldn't you know? I banged my hand on the wheel. Savagely, I pushed the gearshift into Reverse, muttering to myself, "Why did I come back to this stupid town, anyway?"

I'd intended to find Pat Bennington. I wanted to ask her what had really gone on, if anything, between Dottie and Hank, but after Vera and Benjamin I was emotionally wrung out. I couldn't face anyone else, especially as I had no idea how to ask the question I wanted answered. It really was none of my business what Dottie did, but Hank's dead body kept reappearing. Discovering who'd killed him and left him in that closet for me to find felt personal. Besides, I didn't like the idea I might be working with a murderer.

I paused at the corner. Left meant home, quiet, solace, dinner, a glass of wine, aspirin. I turned right.

The Little Theater is a pretty prestigious name for a company who performs in a not-very-prestigious location. They rent the old stage and a back room in the American Legion Hall, and use the new auditorium (built in 1975) for rehearsals and performances. They share the building with the county health department, assorted charities, a parks and recreation ballet class in the afternoon and soft aerobics in the morning. The auditorium gets used for all kinds of functions; auctions, church groups, 4-H meetings. The building is usually open, as one of the groups that use it is doing something. If no one from The Little Theater was there, someone would be, and I could find out when, and where, to find Pat.

I found the back door slightly ajar, pushed it open and walked in. Two women, their backs to me, were doing something with what looked like scenery. The younger one I had never seen before. The older one was Pat.

"Hi," I said.

"Ellen." Pat stuck the paintbrush she'd been using back in a can. "This is a surprise. I could have sworn you weren't interested in our group." She laughed, a genuinely pleased laugh, wiped her hand on an old rag and walked toward me. "This is Tina Morgan," she went on, gesturing toward the girl, "who is letting red paint drip on what should be blue sky. Watch out, Tina, you're ruining the sunset."

"Oh. Sorry." The girl didn't do anything about the red blob, but she did put the paintbrush down. "Say, aren't you the one who found Hank Sawyer the other day?"

I nodded, admitting I was indeed the one, and took a second look at Tina. She'd probably started off pretty, but somewhere along the way she developed a Madonna look-alike complex. Or maybe Lady GaGa. No. Her breasts weren't pointed enough. Very bleached hair, light brown eyes so circled with makeup a raccoon would have fainted with envy, eyelashes coated thick with mascara and a bright red mouth. Her T-shirt was the stretch kind that doesn't quite reach the waist, but her jeans were so tight she couldn't have tucked anything in anyway. I was fascinated, and almost missed the rest of Pat's introduction.

"Tina was in the drama club all through high school." Pat's voice and eyes both showed amusement as I continued to stare at Tina. "She's majoring in design at Arlington Community College, and helps us with scenery and costumes. She's very talented."

Yeah, but at what? I thought. I said, "I'm sure she is."

"I read about it in the paper." Tina ignored my scrutiny and stared at me just as intently. "They said his head was bashed in and there was blood everywhere. Is that true?"

I admitted it was.

"Weren't you scared?" Tina's voice was tinged with awe. "I woulda been. Suppose the murderer had come back?"

"I was terrified." Bless the child; she had provided me with the opening I needed. "Especially after I recognized him. Poor Hank. It must be awful for all of you, too. He was a member of The Little Theater, wasn't he?"

My innocent-seeming question wasn't fooling Pat, who looked at me with one eyebrow raised, but Tina was ready to tell all.

"Oh, yes, and we're all going to miss him. Hank was so much fun." She paused, and took a deep breath. Little tears formed, and I thought about handing her a tissue, but was afraid it would get stuck on one of her gooey lashes. "I can't believe he's really gone," Tina went on. "Why, just last week, he stayed late to help me paint scenery." She thought about that for a minute, then gave a soft giggle.

Pat looked chagrined. "A first, I'm sure."

Tina said, "Huh?"

I wasn't quite sure what to say. I wanted to laugh, but that wouldn't keep the conversation going. "Hank seems to have had quite a reputation. Was it…"

"Deserved?" Pat asked, a little sharply.

"Look, I'm not trying to pry," I said, trying to sound reasonable, "but Aunt Mary said something, and I work with Dottie, and, well, I thought…"

I was having trouble finishing a sentence, but it didn't matter, because Tina jumped right in.

"Hank and Dottie sure were seeing a lot of each other lately. That was kinda strange. She doesn't seem his type."

"Hank was married. He wasn't supposed to have a type."

Tina looked at Pat pityingly. "Dottie sure seemed to like all that attention. Did you know Hank took her home the other night?"

"Yes," Pat and I answered together.

"Did you know he was sitting with her at the bar in the bowling alley? He bought her a drink. They had their heads together, whispering and talking real serious. Come to think of it, Dottie didn't look so happy that night."

"How do you know?" Pat asked her.

"I bowl there."

"Tina, for heaven's sake, that's gossip," Pat said sternly. She looked a little sick. "Do me a favor, go to the office and get some of our brochures for Ellen. Please."

Tina went off with obvious reluctance and Pat turned to me. "Mary told you," she said sadly.

"Yes. She's worried, too. But none of this means Dottie— I can't see her— Oh, for Pete's sake, just because she and Hank had drinks doesn't mean she slept with him. Or murdered him."

"I know. What she and Hank did doesn't concern me. But if he led her on, then jilted her, she's

the type to feel betrayed, desperate. She's so—
vulnerable."

Dottie's anxious face came to mind, and I nodded slowly. "I see what you mean. She'd have
a hard time being dumped." I was thinking of
what I'd gone through after Brian had dumped
me, what I was still going through. God knew I
wasn't tough, but I was lots tougher than Dottie.

"It happened to her before, you know," Pat told
me, "and it took her a long time to come around."

She didn't have a chance to say more. Tina was
back with a handful of information about The Little Theater group, and they insisted on showing
me everything.

I left, thinking amateur theater might be more
fun than I'd thought. Pat had invited me to their
meeting Friday night, and I found myself considering going. I also found myself wondering how
Dan would look in tights.

It was too late to go back to the office. I didn't
want to anyway, so I stopped off at the new supermarket and finally headed home.

I called Aunt Mary while I fed Jake and put
away groceries. She wanted to know how Vera
was doing, agreed Benjamin acted worse every
day and refused to talk about Dottie's possible
love life.

"Are you and Dan coming for dinner tomorrow?"

"I haven't talked to him," I said, "but I'll be there, even if he's not."

"Are you going to Hank's funeral?"

"I don't know." I hadn't thought about the actual funeral. "When is it?"

"Tomorrow, one o'clock, at St. Stephen's. I think you should go. Everyone else will be there."

I thought about it as I hung up. Was there any reason not to go? I thought about it as I put a chicken breast in the oven. I couldn't think of a reason not to go as I fixed a salad, and found several in favor. So, tomorrow, one o'clock, at St. Stephen's Episcopal Church, even though I'd never really known him alive, I would be among Hank Sawyer's mourners.

FIFTEEN

ABOUT EIGHT O'CLOCK, the phone rang.

"Ellie?" The voice was familiar.

"Hi. I wondered what happened to you."

"I've been around," Dan said, "and I hear you have been too."

There was something in his voice I knew I didn't like. "What are you talking about?"

"I hear you've been running around today, playing detective." Uh-oh. His voice sounded grim.

"I have no idea what you mean." I let my own voice become dignified and distant.

"Weren't you out visiting everybody you could think of, asking all kinds of questions?"

"I was out, yes, but if you consider a condolence call to the Sawyers' playing detective, you're reaching."

"I suppose you were representing your family." There was a definite touch of bitterness in that sentence.

"Yes. My mother asked me to."

"I suppose you were shopping at the Emporium because you developed a sudden need for underwear."

"I think we can leave my underwear out of this discussion." I was almost overcome with a desire to laugh. Dan sounded so serious.

"And a crazy desire to become Helen Hayes sent you off to The Little Theater."

"Pat invited me. It looks interesting. Have you ever tried it? You'd look great in tights."

There was a long pause. "I never could win an argument with you," he said with a sigh. "Listen to me, Ellie. This is serious. Don't play detective. You aren't Kinsey Millhone, this isn't one of your blasted books and you could get hurt."

"Who would want to hurt me?" That sentence took me completely by surprise. "I just got back into town, I don't know anyone, or anything."

"Ellie, you found a dead man. A murdered dead man. You missed the murderer by not very much. If whoever killed Hank thinks you saw something, or know something, that's how you could get hurt."

"Oh." I hadn't thought of that.

"This person doesn't panic easily, and is probably pretty ruthless, so I want you to lay off, okay?"

I wasn't going to dignify that with an answer. I hadn't done anything. Yet. Instead I asked, "What do you mean, 'doesn't panic.' How do you know that?"

Dan sighed again. "I'm only telling you this so you won't go off half-cocked, like you used to.

Most of the trouble I got into when we were kids was over some scheme you thought up."

I started to protest, but wasn't about to be side-tracked. "Explain about panicking, or not panicking, please."

"Hank was initially hit in the bedroom. He may have been standing on the tarp, or just close to it, because there's not much blood there. What there was got wiped up with newspaper."

"I didn't see any newspaper."

"It was stuffed behind him in the closet. Anyway, he was hit again, and probably killed, while in the closet. That means a lot of blood. Whoever did it had blood on himself, especially on his legs and shoes. The killer took off his shoes in the closet and walked out of there in stocking feet. A pretty clearheaded person to think of footprints at a time like that."

"Ugh." I could feel a shudder run through my whole body. "Somehow that makes it even more awful."

"Exactly." Dan seemed satisfied he'd gotten his point across. "Which is why…"

"I heard you."

"I wonder," he said. "That brings me to a question. You were in your office that Sunday afternoon, until you got the phone call to show the house. Right?"

I agreed it was, wondering what difference it made. It was after I left that was important.

"Nicole Chambers was with you, but Tom wasn't?"

"Yes. Tom was out previewing houses."

"When did he get back?"

"Right before the phone call. I remember because he came in shaking rain off his glasses, saying it was starting to drizzle. It didn't really start until I got to the bridge."

"What did he have on?" Dan asked.

"Have on? You mean, what was he wearing?"

"Yes, what was he wearing?"

"What difference does that make?"

"Ellie, just answer me, please." It was obvious he was trying to be patient.

I had to think. Tom wore jeans and a sweatshirt to my house that evening. Had he worn them earlier? I thought so. "Jeans," I said firmly, "and a sweatshirt. He didn't have clients, he was only previewing."

"Jeans," Dan repeated. "Not much shows up on jeans. Anything else?"

"What else would…" I was thinking of feet, shoes, new shoes. Tom, walking into my house, showing off his truly ugly new running shoes, the ones he hadn't waited until Monday to buy. Had he had them on when he returned to the office? I couldn't remember. I'd been so excited and nervous about having my first client that Tom's wardrobe hadn't made an impression. But surely it would have if he'd been dripping blood.

"What, Ellie? Why did you stop?"

"It's nothing important," I said, as slowly as possible. There was no way I could get out of mentioning those shoes, but I sure didn't want to. "Only—well—Tom bought some new shoes sometime during the afternoon. He showed them to us when he and Nicole came over."

"Did he have them on when he returned to the office?"

"I have no idea, but I'm sure he wasn't bloody. That I would have remembered."

"New shoes, my, my. What did he do with the old ones?"

"I didn't ask him. Dan, you can't possibly suspect Tom Chambers!"

"I didn't say I did," he said in a much too cheerful voice, "but we have to look at everything. Now, I understand we have an invitation to dinner tomorrow night. I'll pick you up a little before six, and Ellie, just do real estate tomorrow, okay? Nothing else."

He hung up. So did I, a little harder than was necessary. How did he know we'd been invited to dinner at Aunt Mary's? How did he know where

I'd been today? Was Tom really a suspect? It
seemed like I was collecting a whole lot of questions. I stared at the silent phone and vowed I'd get
answers tomorrow night at Aunt Mary's.

SIXTEEN

IT WAS COLD. Outside my bedroom window the sky was Wedgwood blue, and I could see light frost on the lawn and fence posts. Winter wasn't ready to let us off the hook quite yet.

Eyes only half-open, coffee in hand, I rummaged through my closet. I was to attend my first Multiple Listing Service meeting, and felt obliged to look professional, whatever that meant, and what I wore this morning was going to Hank's funeral as well. I chose a long tweed wool skirt, a tunic sweater that belted loosely at the waist, and grabbed my winter coat. One last sip of coffee, an admonition to Jake to behave himself, and I was gone.

Once a week all the Realtors who belong to the Multiple Listing Service have a meeting. They announce their sales, tell about price changes or other information about their listings, pitch the virtues of their respective properties, get caught up on the newest laws designed to drive their clients crazy and them out of business and, finally, preview all the new properties on the market. This would be pretty easy if it were confined to houses in town, but since over half the sales made around here are either small or large ranches, it takes a lot longer and is a lot more complicated.

No one from my office had shown up. I was getting a little nervous when two old pros, friends of my parents, took pity on me and invited me to ride with them. I was delighted, as I didn't trust my memory to take me over winding country roads without getting lost, and I needed an update on our changing agriculture. In fields where I remembered cows and calves, there were grape vines, many with wineries, most with large, new homes. Where I was sure barley once grew, horses grazed, beautiful horses with huge, impressive barns in the background. Here and there I spotted a racetrack. More new homes surveyed the pastures; smaller homes nestled close to the barns.

When I was growing up the only homes were farmhouses, utilitarian and comfortable. Aunt Martha, another of my mother's sisters, was married to a farmer, and we spent many hours at her house, my sister, my cousins and I, chasing chickens, trying to rope baby calves, playing hide-and-seek in the hay barn. The adults sat on the porch or on lawn chairs under the old elm, drinking beer and lemonade, settling the affairs of the country and their neighbors and occasionally yelling at us to "stop that." The dinners we ate came largely from my aunts' and my mother's gardens, and no one would have dreamed of producing a "store-bought" cake.

Bo Chutsky and Madelaine O'Rourke have lived here all their lives. Both have been in real estate for as long as anyone can remember. Bo says he's retiring this year. Madelaine looks real interested when the subject comes up. Between them, they know every house, every ranch and every family in the county. Bo's gotten pretty heavy over the years, to the point where belts alone no longer serve; it's suspenders all the way. He moves around a little slower, but he thinks as fast as ever. Madelaine's flaming red hair, about as real as Lucille Ball's, and her razor-sharp tongue scare most people to death. I think she likes it that way. I hoped I'd get lucky and she'd retire before I had her on the other end of a deal.

Madelaine drove, Bo sat in the passenger seat and I got the back. Almost immediately the conversation turned to murder.

"Terrible thing, you finding Hank like that, Ellen," Bo said. "You all right?"

"I am now. It was pretty awful, though."

Madelaine made a little clicking sound, I guessed of sympathy. "I can't believe it happened. Hank Sawyer, of all people. Murdered. In this town."

"I thought Hank had a reputation for—" I wasn't sure how to finish.

"Say it right out, Ellen. Hank was a woman chaser. We all knew that, but he wasn't a pushy one." Madelaine issued that observation firmly.

"What?" I was startled both by her description and her candor.

Bo laughed. "She means if you told Hank to get lost, he did. He only played with willing partners. Basically, Hank was a good man and, if you leave his little weakness aside, an honest one."

"Then you don't think it was some jealous husband?" I was thinking of Tom.

"More likely someone like Ray Yarbourough. Not that I'm accusing Ray," Madelaine said hurriedly, "but I heard Hank tell Mildred Watson he finally had the goods on Ray, and this time, he was going to make sure Ray lost his license."

"What did Ray do?" I leaned over the front seat a little. Ray made me nervous and I didn't want to miss one word of Madelaine's assessment.

"Honey, what didn't Ray do." She sighed. "He's been bending the law since I met him, but somehow he always seems to slide out from under. Why Sharon keeps him…"

"Loyalty to her father's memory." Bo grunted a little and eased his seat belt away from his belly.

"Smart girl, Sharon. She's done a great job with that business since Hal died."

"Maybe so, but one of these days, Ray Yarbourough's going to get himself in real trouble. I hope he doesn't drag Sharon down with him." Madelaine's voice was grim. "Here we are, first house on our list. Ellen, take notes. You'll never remember unless you do. Now, make this quick, you two. We've got to be back in town early. We've got a funeral to go to."

We finished the houses in town and headed out to the country before the subject of Stop N Shop came up.

"Sharon's done a bang-up job." Bo nodded his admiration. "I thought she'd lost her mind when she put that partnership together to buy that land. She asked me if I wanted to buy in. I didn't, and now I'm kicking myself. That was…when was that, Madelaine?"

"A little more than two years ago." Madelaine slowed down, peering at dirt roads. "That place is around here somewhere."

"Down around that bend." Bo leaned forward as much as his stomach and seat belt would allow. "Turn by that oak tree." He didn't miss a beat getting back to Stop N Shop. "Then, only a few months ago, Sharon comes up with the Stop N

Shop people. Couldn't believe it. 'Course, it's thrown some folks into a tailspin."

"And rightly so," Madelaine said with a sniff. "Not that I don't want that store, I get pretty sick of the Emporium, but some of the downtown people won't survive. I just hope the downtown does."

"What do you mean?" Dan had said something like this, but what could happen to a whole downtown?

"If enough big chains come into a town, everybody goes there and the downtown falls apart." Madelaine slowed some more and deftly drove around a pothole. "People like choices and low prices. Small merchants can't provide either. It takes a lot of planning to keep a small town looking and feeling like one. Here we are."

The subject changed abruptly as Madelaine turned slowly up a dirt road. "Are you sure this is the right place?" she asked Bo, eyeing the washboard road dubiously.

"That's what the directions say, and there's the sign."

"How much do they want for this? How many acres did you say?"

Bo supplied the information. Madelaine snorted in disgust. "They're out of their minds. Well, we're here now. Might as well take a look."

It was on the way back I brought up Benjamin.

"Do you think Stop N Shop would drive the Emporium out of business?"

"Benjamin doesn't need Stop N Shop for that," Bo answered grimly.

"Benjamin's a perfect example of what we were talking about," Madelaine said. "He won't listen to anyone, he's run that business into the ground and is determined to blame it on a new store that isn't even built."

"It sounded like he blamed everything on Hank."

"That, too." There was sadness in Bo's voice, but a trace of disgust as well. "Hank and Benjamin were friends, but after Rose died things sort of fell apart for Benjamin, and he started to blame anything, or anybody, for his troubles."

"He's led the opposition to that store right from the beginning." Madelaine slowed down as we approached my office, then stopped the car with a jerk.

"Benjamin attacked Hank with a hammer." I'd opened the back door but paused, waiting to see if there was a response.

"I know," Madelaine said softly. She glanced at Bo, who was looking straight ahead, saying nothing. "I know," she repeated.

SEVENTEEN

I WALKED INTO a full office. Ray was in the conference room with a young couple. Tom was on the phone, making notes on a legal pad as he talked. Nicole stood beside the copying machine, running something, and Sharon sat at her desk, intently going through a file of papers. Dottie was busy at the computer, as usual.

"Any messages?" I got the answer I expected.

"No." She didn't look away from the screen.

I walked by Nicole to get to the coffeemaker.

"Are you and Tom going to the funeral?"

"Yes."

If conversations got any shorter, we'd all be communicating in sign language.

"Want to ride with me?"

"Oh, Ellen, thanks." Nicole looked at me for the first time. "I have a terrible headache. I think we're going straight home after the service."

Actually, I was glad to go alone. I'd only offered to be polite. I took a better look at Nicole and wondered what had happened. She looked like a deflated balloon. Bouncy, bubbly Nicole was dragging.

"Are you sick?" Flu, colds, it was the right time of year.

"Sick," she repeated, looking over at Tom. "Not with anything contagious."

Tom didn't look any better than Nicole. What was the matter with them? Surely they weren't worried Tom might be a suspect. If they were, they were advertising it for the entire world to see. No. Tom wouldn't, couldn't, commit murder. Something's going on, though, I thought, but whatever it is, they weren't making it any better slinking around looking guilty.

I picked through the coffee mugs, looking for a clean one, settled for one that looked passable, filled it and headed for my own desk. There, on my calendar, marked in red, it said, "floor time." We are a small office and try to take turns making sure someone is available to answer inquiries on properties, both from other agents and potential clients. This afternoon, it was my turn.

I walked over to Dottie's desk. "I'm on the floor this afternoon and I really…"

"Don't worry, Ellen." She actually looked up at me. "We're closing the office. Hank was a good client, and a good friend to most of us. Sharon wants all of us there." She gave a little sniff.

"You'd known Hank a long time." I wasn't sure what else to say. Should I offer condolences?

"A long time." There was a lot of emotion in Dottie's voice, but I couldn't sort it out. "Hank was a client of Sharon's father. I was secretary then, too." She gave a deep, wobbly sort of sigh. "We were in The Little Theater group together. He was a fine man."

I wanted to ask her if she'd been having an affair with him, but obviously I couldn't. However, since we were talking about The Little Theater group... "I understand Hank used to give you a ride home from the meetings." I tried not to sound intrusive, just sympathetic. "And that he sometimes took you bowling."

"Bowling?" Dottie's head jerked up like it had been yanked. "What do you mean?"

"Nothing." I was surprised and embarrassed I'd caused this reaction. "Only, someone said they saw you together at the bowling alley."

"I hate small towns." She looked toward Sharon's office with a more than normally anxious expression. "Does Sharon know?"

"I have no idea." I kept my voice low; I wasn't sure why, except Dottie's concern Sharon might hear was contagious. "I won't mention it again. I'm real sorry, Dottie, I didn't mean to upset you."

Evidently I had the answer to my question.

Dottie and Hank had been doing something they didn't want made public, and Dottie sure didn't want Sharon to find out. Was she afraid she'd be fired?

"Thanks, and, Ellen? Do you think maybe we could talk? There's something…"

"Ellen." Sharon's voice came from directly over my shoulder. "I'm glad you're here. Are you going to Hank's funeral?"

"Yes. I had floor duty, but Dottie says we're closing the office." I hoped Sharon hadn't seen me jump. I felt like a kid caught whispering in class.

Sharon looked at me sharply, then down at Dottie, but all she said was, "I'm going to do some errands, then go to lunch. I'll see all of you at the church."

"Sharon," Dottie said hurriedly, "those addresses I needed. Did you get them yet?"

Sharon stopped, turned and looked down at Dottie. "I'm sure I already told you." Sharon's voice was much too patient. Dottie flushed. "You don't have to worry about that. I have all that information on my own computer, and I've taken care of everything." She gave Dottie a long look, me a shorter one, shifted her big bag higher up her shoulder, straightened out her black cashmere sweater and left.

"She's so damned efficient." Dottie's voice was

low with an underlay of—what? The only thing I could tell was that I was surprised, no, shocked, that mousy Dottie would use an expletive. Maybe Dottie had hidden depths. But she was asking me a question and my attention to it left her depths, hidden or otherwise, unexplored.

"Ellen, if you're not busy tonight, maybe you'd like to come to my house for a glass of wine, or something."

I was surprised again, and touched. "I can't tonight, but I'd love to some other time."

"Sure." She looked whipped and guilt immediately struck. This is ridiculous, I thought crossly. I'm going home to lunch where the only one I have to deal with is Jake.

Ray emerged from the conference room, shepherding his young couple toward the door.

"You're doing the right thing," he told them, oozing confidence. "That house is a great buy. You'll be real happy there."

They didn't look entirely convinced. "You're sure about the plumbing?" The woman, girl really, asked somewhat tentatively. "And the roof. Shouldn't we have it checked? It looks pretty old."

"We don't have many to choose from, do we," Ray replied heartily. "Town this size, in your price range. Besides, the whole town is old."

"I suppose." The girl sounded doubtful and there were worry lines across her forehead.

"I'll let you know, but I'm sure this offer will be accepted. Now, you've got that appointment with the lender, and you don't want to be late. I'll call you." He almost shoved them out the door.

"First-time home buyers," he said, unnecessarily. "Don't have any money, but expect a mansion."

"I thought we were supposed to encourage inspections." I was caught off guard by Ray's attitude.

"All inspections do is foul up a deal." Ray looked at me with a sour expression that somehow had a warning in it. "Those kids'll be fine."

Tom and Nicole had come up behind Ray, coats on, ready to leave. The distaste on Tom's face as he listened to Ray was plain, but he didn't say anything.

"We're leaving now," Nicole told Dottie. "I don't think we'll be back after the funeral, so could you put everything on our voice mail?"

Dottie nodded and watched them start toward the door. "Tom, you're going to do what we agreed, aren't you?" She looked at him anxiously.

Tom stopped and slowly turned back. He looked as if he wanted to say something, but Ray was hanging on every word. "For a while." He pointedly ignored Ray and hurried after Nicole.

"What was that all about?" Ray turned back toward Dottie, his voice and his eyes filled with curiosity.

Dottie ignored him. She shut down her computer and tidied up her desk.

"I've got this file, with this offer." Belligerence was back. "If you're leaving, what am I going to do with it?"

"Put it there, with all the other working offers." Dottie actually let a little irritation show. "That's where you always put them. There's nothing I can do until it's accepted."

Ray growled a little, but slipped the file into the slot Dottie had indicated.

"Are you going to the funeral?" I asked, more to ease the tension than because I cared. It didn't work.

"What do you think I am, a hypocrite?" Ray transferred his irritation to me and snarled. "Hank hated me, he was out to get me, and didn't care how many lies he told to do it. You think I'm going to his funeral and pretend I'm sad he's dead? I don't think so." He stalked back to his desk, grabbed his briefcase, then came back past us and went out the door without another word.

"Ouch."

"Yeah." Dottie nodded her agreement. "I'm going to lock up, Ellen. Unless there's something…"

"No, no. I'm going. See you later." I grabbed my purse and headed for home.

EIGHTEEN

THE STREETS AROUND St. Stephen's were filled with cars. I finally found a place behind First Methodist and walked back. I hurried up the steps, a little out of breath and almost late. The church was largely full. Only a few people were still standing out front, trying to ignore the hearse, talking in the hushed tones that somehow seem appropriate for these occasions.

I had always loved this church. My parents had attended Valley Presbyterian, but another aunt had joined St. Stephen's, causing a raised eyebrow or two in the family. I had gone with her a few times and been entranced with the large stained-glass window behind the altar and the ornate choir loft. I stopped briefly to admire the window, grateful that it hadn't changed. An usher approached and I followed him a short way down the aisle to one of the only open seats. There were a lot of people around who nodded, confident I knew them. Most of them were about my parents' age, many looked familiar, but I could put names to only one or two. I didn't see anyone I really knew.

The family took their places, the casket started up the aisle and the service began. Reverend Hanlon's sermon was consoling, the eulogies moving, and the choir did their best. Afterward, everyone milled around in front of the church while the procession to the cemetery was organized. I came out onto the steps in time to see Vera climb into the family limousine, followed by Violet and several others I didn't recognize. I looked around for familiar faces and spotted Dottie standing with a small group off to one side. Tina was there, in a skirt almost long enough to be considered decent, and so was Pat. Ruthie, from the Yum Yum, was patting Dottie gently on the shoulder, while they both daubed their eyes with tissues. Pat saw me, waved and mouthed, "See you at the house later." I waved back and kept edging my way through the crowd. Someone handed me a red "funeral" placard for my windshield. I wondered if I'd make it back to my car in time to use it.

Sharon was standing with the mayor and his wife, talking in low tones to a couple I didn't know. She didn't see me and I didn't stop. I was down the steps when I ran into Tom and Nicole.

"Where's your thing?" I waved my red placard at them. "You'll need it to be in the procession to the cemetery."

"We're not going." Tom slipped his arm around

Nicole's shoulder and pulled her a little closer. "Nicole's headache is worse, and I've got some work to do. We're going to head home."

I watched them walk away, wondering again what was going on. They had given statements to the police, but so had everybody else who'd seen Hank in the last forty-eight hours of his life. They acted as if they expected Tom to be arrested any minute, but there was no reason to think that was true. Except for Dan's cryptic questions of last night. I started again toward my car, a little slower and a lot more thoughtfully.

"Hey." A voice sounded in my ear, and a strong hand grabbed me by the arm. I jumped, and gave off a most undignified squeal.

"You are one jumpy female." Dan Dunham laughed down at my furious face.

"Don't do that!"

"Don't do what?" He was all innocence. "I'll be there at six. Be ready. Mary likes to eat on time."

"You already told me when you'd be there, and I'm never late."

"Yeah? Then you've changed a lot." He grinned again at me and left.

"Wait," I called after him. "What are you doing here? What…"

Dan raised his hand in a little wave, but didn't

turn around, and I lost sight of him as he rounded the corner.

"He is the most infuriating— He hasn't changed. Not one bit!" I said that loud enough so several others headed for their cars glanced at me. I got to mine, threw the red placard on the dash, gunned the engine a little and eased my way into the procession.

NINETEEN

THE CEMETERY IS on the outskirts of town, built on a gently sloping hillside. The graves date back to the early eighteen hundreds. It's a beautiful place, serene and dignified. Huge oaks are much in evidence, set off by perfectly manicured grounds. The afternoon sky had turned slate-gray and a cold light seemed to surround the marble angels, crosses and saints that dominated this old part of the cemetery. The casket, guided on its trolley by the pallbearers, bumped and swayed as it made its way over the grass to the empty grave. I pulled my coat closer around me as I watched.

Vera sat in one of the folding chairs, flanked by her family, a shrunken figure swathed in black. She held on to Violet with one hand. With the other she held a handkerchief to her face. She kept staring at the casket, now resting quietly on the green fake grass. I didn't think she heard the prayers being offered or saw the pall bearers lined up, Benjamin on one end.

I saw him. I couldn't take my eyes off him. He had on a badly fitting dark blue suit, a white shirt whose collar was too big, and a snap-on bow tie, hanging down a little on one side. But it wasn't his clothes that held my attention. It was the expression that kept creeping over his face. Sorrowful, except for a little smirk of self-satisfaction that kept peeking out. He'd quickly tuck it away behind the mask of mourner, but it was there. Only, what did it mean?

The graveside prayers were finished, Vera was led away and the crowd drifted back toward their cars. I walked toward mine when I felt someone clutch my arm. It was Sharon.

"Sorry, Ellen. It's this blasted grass. My heel caught." Her face, white above her black cashmere sweater, showed strain her makeup couldn't hide.

"Are you going back to the house?"

"Do we have a choice?" She walked toward her car.

I got into mine and joined the slow-moving line out of the cemetery gates. The exodus to the Sawyer house had begun.

Custom in our town dictates that everyone who attends a funeral and burial troop back to the family home and offer one more set of condolences. The neighbor ladies serve the tons of food that have been pouring in, and the men stand around and swap outrageous tales about the dead person. I wondered what they were going to say about Hank.

The street was filled with vehicles when I arrived, about half of them pickups. Lots of the men filing into the house were dressed in clean, pressed jeans, Western-style cotton shirts, boots and parkas. The signs on the trucks advertised plumbing, framing, electrical, concrete work, all kinds of construction. Hank's friends had turned out in force. There were a few people leaving, but more were arriving as I walked up to the door. The dining room buzzed with conversation, and the aroma of tuna casserole and coffee hung in the air. I knew there would be beer on the back porch. Lots of full plates would find their way to the backyard where cans would be popped and cigarettes lit.

A woman slightly older than Violet stopped me at the front door. "You're Ellen McKenzie, aren't you." She held out her hand.

I nodded, and shook hers weakly. This must be the other daughter, but I had no idea what her name was.

"I didn't get a chance to thank you for looking in on Mother yesterday. It meant so much to her." She gave my hand a little squeeze before she dropped it. "Mother's in the living room if you'd like to speak to her again."

I couldn't think of anything I would like less, nor could I imagine why Vera would want to see me, or, for that matter, any of the cast of thousands milling through her house. However, some things you can't get out of, so into the living room I went.

She was sitting in the same chair as yesterday, only this time she was surrounded by people. I watched from the doorway for a moment as the faces of the group around her changed. Vera seemed only marginally aware of any of them, still hugging her private grief around her like a shawl. The line moved slowly, people awkwardly giving her a little pat, murmuring something. Occasionally someone leaned down to brush her with a kiss. The Little Theater people had already passed through when it was my turn to pat her gently on the shoulder and speak words in her ear that had no meaning.

Duty done, I headed for the coffee and the cups piled up at the end of the extended table. Dottie was there with Pat, who gave me a warm smile.

"Hi. I was telling Dottie about your visit yesterday. We're all hoping you'll join our group. We have great things planned, and I know you'd have fun." Pat handed me a full coffee cup.

I smiled, saying I'd think about it, but my mind wasn't on The Little Theater. I didn't think Dottie's was either. She looked more anxious than ever, and was absently shredding a napkin into her saucer.

"Do you want something to eat, Ellen?" She

scooped the napkin remains into a trash bag placed at the end of the table. "There's all kinds of things here. I could get you a plate…"

"If you spoil your dinner," said a voice behind us, "you just could be in trouble."

Aunt Mary joined our group, acknowledging us all with a regal bob of her head. "Ellen's bringing Dan to dinner at my house tonight, and I expect appetites to match my efforts."

Dottie and Pat exchanged knowing looks, which I ignored. Instead I stared, captivated, at Aunt Mary's hat. I'd never seen anything like it outside of old 1930's movies. Had she kept it all that time? Or was it another legacy of the perennial church rummage sales?

Aunt Mary caught me staring at it. "If you like it so much, Ellen," she said, reaching a hand up to touch the brim, "I'll let you borrow it sometime. Don't forget. Six-thirty. Sharp!" She swooped up a tray of dirty cups and left.

Pat walked off, chuckling, and Dottie turned to join the conversation of the group behind us. Left alone, I emptied my cup and looked around for a refill. I glanced at the doorway to see Vera, a daughter on each side, head down the hall toward the bedrooms. *Poor thing,* I thought, *she must be exhausted.*

Evidently I wasn't the only one who noticed her

leave, for the quiet hum of conversation immediately got louder.

I filled my cup, picked up a brownie and turned to find myself standing with Benjamin and several of the other downtown storeowners.

"It's terrible about Hank, just terrible," Benjamin was saying around a mouthful of potato salad, "but it'll be the end of that blasted Stop N Shop."

"Why?" I asked. I got a scornful look.

"Hank was the drivin' force behind gettin' that store okayed, and, as much as we'll all miss him, now we can get that damn store stopped!"

"What are you saying?" I lowered my coffee cup onto the plate where the brownie was and immediately splashed coffee on it. I almost didn't notice. My attention was on what Benjamin had just said, or rather, implied. "That somehow Hank's death and the new store are connected?"

"Now, well, don't you go puttin' words in my mouth," Benjamin sputtered, spraying us all with cookie crumbs. "Everyone knew it was Hank that wanted that store. He said he wouldn't vote, but he was puttin' the pressure on, just the same. Said it was good for the town. What he really meant, it was good for Hank!"

The other members of our little group looked around, embarrassed. They started drifting away. I didn't blame them. Accusing a man of manipulating city government for his own profit, in that man's own home, especially at that man's funeral, could hardly be considered good manners.

I hadn't seen Sharon come up. She set her cup and saucer carefully on the table before she spoke to Benjamin. Her voice was low but sharp. "Of course Hank wanted that store. It represents progress, growth. If you and your cronies had your way, we'd all shrivel up and blow away."

"It's only progress if it makes you money," Benjamin spat out. His Adam's apple was bobbing up and down under his loose shirt collar. "You, Hank and all the rest of them partners of yours'll make a profit. The rest of us'll go broke!"

"That's ridiculous." Exasperation was clearly etched on Sharon's face. "A new store will bring shoppers in from all over the county. Hank knew that. He believed in that store, he believed in what we are trying to do, he— Dottie, what is it?"

Dottie had edged into the group and was trying to interrupt. I was astonished. I'd never seen her do anything that brave. She wrung her hands and her face was flushed, but she took a deep breath and out it came.

"Hank was beginning to have doubts."

"What?" Sharon's face paled. "What are you talking about?"

"What kind of doubts?"

Sharon glanced at me out of the corner of her eye, then zeroed in on Dottie. "He didn't have any doubts. He thought that store was a wonderful idea."

"He was beginning to change his mind." It must have been hard for her, but Dottie held her ground. "The last time I talked to him he said he was taking a long look at the whole Stop N Shop thing."

The expression on Benjamin's face changed so quickly I couldn't guess what he was thinking. "That's what he said? Word for word?"

"As close as I can remember. He didn't make an issue of it, only mentioned it in passing." Dottie's voice faded away along with her courage. She looked at Sharon's stony face, and I was pretty sure she wished she'd kept her mouth shut.

"Takin' a long look could mean anything. Doesn't mean he'd changed his mind. Probably was still in favor of the whole thing." Benjamin had no intention of abandoning his position. "When did all this happen, anyway? I talked to him last weekend and didn't see any signs he'd changed his mind."

"Yes, Dottie." There was ice in Sharon's voice. "When did you have this conversation with Hank?"

"I don't know." Dottie had started to stammer. "A few days ago. Maybe he was still in favor, maybe he meant something else." She started to back out of the group, hit the edge of the table and grabbed a coffee cup just in time to keep it from crashing to the floor. "Oh, oh dear." She looked as if she could break into tears any moment. "I, ah, I'd better go. Are you going back to the office, Sharon?" Her eyes were on the floor, the wall, the chandelier, everywhere but any of us.

"No," Sharon said. "No, I'm not."

"Well, well then, I guess I'll see you tomorrow." She turned and fled.

"Silly woman." Benjamin's voice was full of scorn.

"We agree on that." It was obvious she meant it was the only thing on which they agreed.

Benjamin glared at Sharon, included me and stalked off toward the backyard, apparently looking for a more receptive audience for his diatribe against Stop N Shop.

"He gets worse every day." Sharon sighed. She set her coffee cup down on the table, shaking her head.

"He's pretty bad." But it wasn't Benjamin I wanted to talk about. "Sharon, about Dottie. I'm sure she didn't mean…"

"I know." She rubbed her hand over her eyes. "I know. I shouldn't get so impatient with her, but she's so—so— What was she doing hanging around Hank, anyway?"

I shrugged. I didn't think she expected an answer, and I wasn't about to provide one.

"I think Dottie had the right idea." I set my own coffee cup down. "I'm going home."

"Of course." Sharon smiled a little. "You and Dan are going to dinner at Mary's, aren't you?"

How did you know that? I wanted to scream. Instead I nodded, smiled a little myself, bid Vera a silent farewell and left.

TWENTY

THE CLOCK STRUCK six and the doorbell rang. Had he been waiting on the porch, counting down the seconds? It hadn't worked. I was ready.

"It's a beautiful night. Look at all those stars. Let's walk."

"It's darn near freezing. You can see the stars through the windshield."

We drove.

As we walked up on Aunt Mary's front porch, Dan's expression changed. He began to get that dreamy, wistful look common to men and dogs when they smell a really good dinner. I couldn't blame him. The aroma of roasting pork with sage was enough to make anyone salivate. If tradition held, there would be homemade applesauce, pan-roasted potatoes and dark, rich gingerbread with lemon sauce. Tradition held.

Aunt Mary met us at the door. I almost laughed at the expression on Dan's face. Aunt Mary has never been one for home decorating. Everything she has she either inherited or picked up at the church rummage sales she runs, and she sees no need to color co-ordinate it. She wears her church sale clothes with the same disregard for fashion or figure. As children, we hadn't noticed. As adults, the results were sometimes unsettling. Tonight she had outdone herself. She had on an ankle-length caftan with every color of the rainbow splashed on it with no attempt at pattern. Under that, she had on what looked like tights of some sort, and moccasins. The aftermath of an earthquake in a paint factory came to mind.

Dan collected himself quickly and, to his credit, didn't laugh. Good thing. Aunt Mary's dinners are no laughing matter.

During dinner, we kept the conversation to reminiscences, exploring the funny, and not so funny, memories of childhood, catching each other, and Aunt Mary, up on family and telling each other a little about the events that had brought us both back to Santa Louisa. Dan spoke tenderly, but briefly, of his wife and son. Time had covered over some of the pain, but much still remained, and my heart went out to him. I told him about Susannah, the only good thing to come out of my marriage to Dr. Brian McKenzie. "My college graduation and Susannah were in a race to the finish line," I said, laughing somewhat ruefully at the memory. "Graduation won by two days."

"Whatever happened to that old fur hat you used to wear?" Aunt Mary asked Dan.

"My coonskin hat." Dan smiled at the memory. "I stalked many a bear in that hat. Didn't even mind Ellie calling me Daniel Boone. Then." He looked at me meaningfully.

"You looked silly, running around with a plastic rifle and a rubber knife." I ignored his reference to my resurrecting a childhood name.

"No sillier than you in those tap shoes and that baggy pink leotard."

Now there was a memory I could have done without. When I was about seven, my mother decided I was the next Shirley Temple, and off I went to dance school. She watched me take a few lessons, and mercifully ended the agony for both of us.

It was good to bury the unappetizing taste of town feuds, controversy and murder for a while, but the inevitable happened, and, with dessert, the conversation returned to the present.

Aunt Mary and I cleared the table. Dan refilled the coffee cups and accepted seconds on gingerbread. He drowned it with lemon sauce before he paused to pull a piece of paper out of his pocket.

"Here." He handed it to Aunt Mary. "This is what I wanted you to look at. Tell me about these people."

So! I thought. That's how he knew we were

coming here tonight. He'd been talking to Aunt Mary behind my back.

"I don't know what you want me to tell." Aunt Mary put on her reading glasses and peered at the paper.

"Do you know them?" Dan shoved away his empty plate.

I pushed my chair back and walked around to see what Dan had given her. It was the list of names Dan had shown Sharon, the list of partners that owned the Stop N Shop land. I looked at him inquiringly. Why was he showing it to Aunt Mary?

"Of course I know them. They are all people who've lived in this town for years."

"Even the highlighted ones?"

"Yes. Look, here's the Bullocks." Aunt Mary pointed to one of the names highlighted in yellow. "I talked to Yvonne just the other day. She told me they sold their shares."

"Wasn't she upset they got out, now that Stop N Shop buying the land would have made them so much more money?" Dan sounded only mildly curious, but I wondered.

"Not a bit," Aunt Mary replied. "Yvonne said they made a nice profit. You know, Dan, the people who bought into that partnership were all friends of Sharon's father. After he got sick and she came home to take over the real estate office, lots of people felt, oh, not sorry for her, but sort of worried she wouldn't succeed. When she came up with this idea, most folks figured they were somehow supporting Hal, and they'd be lucky to get their money back." Aunt Mary sighed. "She wanted me to put money in. It wasn't much, no one put up much, but I didn't think I could afford it."

"So you didn't buy in, but these others did." Dan leaned forward a little. "That still doesn't explain why the Bullocks, and all these others, aren't upset."

"Yvonne said Stop N Shop isn't a sure thing. They made a profit, one they hadn't expected, and they're glad to be out."

"I wonder if Alice Ives feels that way," I said.

"Alice." Aunt Mary looked up at me, surprise on her face. "Do you remember her?"

"She called me," I said a little proudly. "I'm going to list her house."

"So she's finally made up her mind." Aunt Mary nodded. "I'm so glad she called you, Ellen. I know you'll do a wonderful job for her."

For the first time, I wondered how Alice knew I was working in real estate, let alone that I was back in town. I took a closer look at Aunt Mary, but her expression gave away nothing.

She handed the list back to Dan. "Why did you want to know about these people?"

"Just curious. Hank had that list in his pocket. It

seemed like a funny thing to be carrying around, and I wondered."

"Wondered what? If Hank also knew all those people? Do you think one of those people some-how…?" I broke off. I had hit a mental dead end.

"I was curious, Ellie. Nothing more." Dan was carefully folding the paper and putting it back in his pocket.

"Who do you think killed Hank?"

"Ellen!" said Aunt Mary. "You can't ask him that."

Why not? I thought. *He asks me questions, and he expects answers.* Aloud I said, "You were asking me questions about Tom Chambers. You don't really suspect him, do you?"

"Now, Ellie." Dan had that old teasing look in his eyes. "You know I can't…"

He was interrupted by Aunt Mary. "What's all this about Tom Chambers?"

"Dan thinks Tom might have killed Hank in a fit of rage because Hank kept hanging around Nicole." I kept my tone innocent and my eye on Dan. "Because he bought new shoes on Sunday."

"What?" Aunt Mary looked first at me. I shrugged. She turned toward Dan. "What are you talking about? Tom didn't kill Hank, he wouldn't. And what's all this about shoes?"

Dan glared at me, but he started to explain.

"Hank was still alive when he was dragged into that closet. He was hit—more than once when he lay on that tarp. Head wounds bleed a lot. There was blood everywhere. If the murderer got blood on his shoes, and it was almost impossible not to, he would have left footprints somewhere. There weren't any, so whoever killed him took his shoes off in that closet and left in his stocking feet."

Aunt Mary looked a little pale. I sympathized.

"What does that have to do with Tom?"

"Tom bought new running shoes on Sunday," I explained. "He came back to the office with them on."

"Where did he get shoes on a Sunday?"

"At that little store those Indian brothers run," I told her, "or maybe they're Pakistani."

"Shows his good sense he didn't wait to shop at the Emporium." She shifted in her chair so that she faced Dan directly. "How can you possibly suspect someone of something as horrible as murder because they bought new shoes?" She used her old "see here, young man" voice, and Dan reacted. I loved it, at least for a minute.

"I didn't say I suspected him, Ellie did. But he does have some explaining to do." He smiled at me over the top of his coffee cup.

"There's more?" Aunt Mary's tone plainly said she doubted it.

"I'm afraid so." Dan set his cup down and reverted from Dan-the-friend back to the policeman Dan. "We collected a lot of fingerprints all over that house. Most were worthless, but we expect that. Some we've identified. Yours, Ellie. Right where you said they'd be. And Harvey's, where he grabbed the closet door."

"Probably to keep himself from fainting," I said cryptically.

"Maybe so." There was a quick flicker of amusement in Dan's eyes. "We also found Tom's on the closet door. Right near the top, where you'd take hold if you were going to pull it open."

"So? Probably half the real estate agents in town have looked at that house. Tom could have left his prints on that door anytime."

"Two problems with that." Dan held up two fingers, pushed the first one down. "First, those prints are over smudged ones, which means they got there after the workmen left, which means over the weekend. Second, Tom swore in his statement he hadn't been near that house for at least two weeks. Makes me wonder."

"So that's why Tom and Nicole have been acting so strange." I thought back to Nicole's headache and Tom's nervousness. "They probably think you're going to arrest him any minute. But you're not, are you?"

"Not right this minute, no." A faint hint of that teasing look was back in his eyes.

"You're not going to arrest him at all," Aunt Mary said. "He didn't do it."

"Tom Chambers has a terrible temper, Mary. You know that. Everyone knows that."

"But he controls it better now." She didn't sound as convinced, or as convincing, as I would have liked. "Besides, Tom doesn't stay mad. He blows up and then it's all over. Oh."

"Yes," Dan said gently. "This wasn't premeditated."

I wasn't listening to them. I was thinking back to this afternoon. Unfortunately, I did it aloud. "I wonder why Dottie said that?" came out before I could stop it.

"Said what?"

"Nothing, nothing at all."

"Ellie," Dan said in a patient, warning voice, "don't do that. What did Dottie say?"

Damn. This was the second time. I was going to have to learn to think quieter. "She told Tom to remember their agreement."

"What agreement? Why did she say that?"

"I haven't any idea." I would have given a lot to take back my unfortunate statement. Too late. "I thought it was strange at the time. So did Ray."

"Ray!" exclaimed Aunt Mary.

Dan gave me the "you'd better give up because I'm not giving in" look. Aunt Mary looked distraught. I was stuck.

"That's really all." I sighed. "We were at the office, and everybody was leaving for the funeral. Tom and Nicole headed out the door, but Dottie stopped them. She said to Tom, 'remember what we agreed,' or something like that. He kind of paused, and said he remembered. Ray wanted to know what she meant, but she wouldn't say."

"Did Tom?"

I hesitated. "No. He got red in the face, but he didn't do anything. Just left."

"But what does it mean?" Aunt Mary got up, poured us all some more coffee, laced hers with cream and stirred it vigorously.

"I don't know." The look on Dan's face was thoughtful and somehow grim. I shivered. "Probably nothing. But, tomorrow morning, Dottie and I just might have coffee and donuts at the Yum Yum."

He looked at his watch, then at Aunt Mary's tired face. "It's nine-thirty. Mary, let us help you with those dishes, then I think we'll clear out of here."

We weren't, of course, allowed to touch a dish and, after telling her several times how wonderful the dinner was and thanking her again, Dan and I were in the car, making the short drive to my house.

Sitting in the passenger seat beside Dan felt natural, as though I'd been doing it for years. *Wait just a darn minute, Ellen McKenzie,* I thought, and as much to distract myself as anything, I asked, "Do you really think Tom's guilty?"

"I don't know, Ellie," Dan said with a little sigh. "I hope not. But then, I don't want it to be anyone I know. Being a policeman in a small town is usually pretty good. But not now."

I didn't say anything more until we were in my driveway. "It wouldn't be so bad if it were Ray."

Dan started to laugh. "No, Ray I'd have an easier time with. Too bad we can't write the final chapter, like they do in those mysteries you used to read. Do you still read those things?"

"Absolutely." I was ready to be defensive, remembering his Nancy Drew jokes.

"Yeah," he said a little tiredly. "Just remember, please, this is real life. Don't play detective."

He reached across me and opened the door. I climbed out, then hesitated a second.

"I'll wait until you get in the door," he said. "Call you tomorrow."

I walked up onto the front porch, opened the door and closed it a little harder than necessary.

What did you expect? I asked myself. I didn't get an answer, but I didn't really want one.

Jake came to greet me, rubbed against my legs, told me his dinner had been inadequate, wouldn't I like to fill his dish again. I wandered into the kitchen, told him he had food, thought about tea, rejected the idea, headed for the TV, decided the ten o'clock news would be too depressing. Bed and my book seemed the only options left.

The red light on my answering machine was blinking. At first I was going to ignore it, but what if it was Susannah, needing me? I pushed the button and there was Dottie.

"Ellen, I know you are out tonight, but could you call me when you get in? Or, if you don't mind, could you come over? I don't know what to do and I so much need to talk to you. I'll be up late."

I stared at the machine, as if it could tell me what that phone call was all about. Why did Dottie want to talk to me? She sounded upset, more than upset. Should I call her? I glanced at my bedside clock. Ten after ten. Too late to go over to her house? No. The way she sounded, phones wouldn't work. But a cup of tea might. I pulled my coat back on and turned to go. A soft purr made me pause. Jake, curled into an orange ball, lay in the middle of my pillow. At least someone around here had some sense.

TWENTY-ONE

I HAD BEEN to Dottie's house only one time, to pick up some papers, and wasn't sure I'd recognize the long, narrow driveway in the dark. I drove down the street, looking for the white picket fence that separated her one-bedroom cottage from the sidewalk. I didn't think I could miss the gate that opened onto the pathway that wound through fruit trees, vegetables, rose bushes and an array of wildly blooming annuals, interspersed with a bird bath and a stone rabbit or two. The effect was charming, as was the cottage. I'd been told that Dottie bought it in terrible condition and did most of the work herself. However anxious and unsure of herself Dottie might be in work and social situations, here she shone. The cottage had a picture-book look, flower-filled white window boxes, white shutters against gray-blue walls, even a watermelon-pink front door.

I missed it the first time, but finally found the driveway and started slowly down. Most of the windows on the street side of Dottie's cottage were dark, only a sliver of blue light from the television showed through a crack in the closed curtains. I stopped in front of her tiny garage, went through the gap in the fence and along the stone path toward the front door.

If she'd wanted me to come so bad, I thought grumpily, she could have left a porch light on. Groping, my hand found the old bellpull she used instead of chimes, and I gave it a yank. Its clang sounded boldly in the night air, loud enough to wake half the neighborhood. Somewhere a dog barked, but there was no answer from inside the house. I hesitated a minute, expecting the porch light to snap on. Nothing. I pulled once more. Again the dog barked, but Dottie didn't answer. I called out, "Dottie, it's me, Ellen," and knocked loudly. Other dogs started to bark, one howled, forming a chorus, but the house stayed silent.

Irritation mixed with alarm. She'd called me, insisted I come. Why wouldn't she answer? I reached down and tried the door handle. Locked. Now what? Should I go home? No, I couldn't. Something was wrong, and I had to find out what it was.

Edging my way through a bush, hoping I wasn't going to end up ankle-deep in mud, I put my eye to the slit in the curtain. I couldn't see much of the room, but I could see another light that probably came from the kitchen. She must be there, but why didn't she answer? The bathroom. Of course. I dislodged myself from the bush, and started around the side of the house. I tripped on something, and muttered some unkind things about Dottie and her refusal to turn on any lights. The night was dark, the stars evidently taking time out, and I was afraid I'd break my neck before I got to the kitchen door.

Finally. The light from her kitchen shone like a beacon through the window and the slightly open back door. I paused for a second, looking at it. It was chilly. No, cold. Why would anyone leave their door open on such a night?

I almost didn't go on. Every nerve ending I owned was shouting, *leave, run, get out of here,* but I had to go on. One foot in front of the other, I slowly approached the door, pulled it open and looked in. The fluorescent lights gave me a clear view of what lay on the black-and-white kitchen floor. I stopped, hand over my mouth, and for a moment forgot to breathe. Dottie. Like a rag doll a child had dropped, she lay on the floor, eyes staring, the front of her yellow sweatshirt stained bright red.

Oh, my God, I thought wildly. *No, this can't be happening. Not again.*

I rushed in, called her name and knelt beside her, but I knew there was no hope. Her open eyes were blank, and no breath disturbed the blood that still dripped slowly from her sweatshirt. I waited for the waves of nausea to subside, then looked around for a phone. There was one on the wall, and with a trembling hand I dialed 911.

I kept trying not to look at her. Sweet, anxious Dottie, what had she wanted to tell me? Who had killed her? Why? She knew something, she must have, but what? I thought about Tom, but pushed the thought away. He wouldn't have done this. Besides, he didn't have a gun, and I was sure Dottie had been shot. All that blood on her front, and a faint trace of cordite in the air convinced me. Who did have a gun? Ray? Benjamin? But why would they want Dottie dead? My hands were clutching the edge of the sink as I waited, and I decided to quit thinking. Dan was right. Real murder wasn't fun.

Sirens screamed, rudely breaking the silence, and my old friend the dog went crazy. He'd have laryngitis by morning. A police car drove into the alley behind Dottie's garage, its lights flashing. Another joined it. An ambulance tried to maneuver down the drive. The fire trucks had a harder time. Dottie's narrow lot wasn't very accommodating, and they were forced to stay on the street. No lack of light in the neighborhood now. Porch lights came on one after another like a switch-board gone berserk.

The first policeman through the door was Gary, the young man who'd taken my statement when I'd found Hank. He gave me a startled look but immediately transferred his attention to poor Dottie. When he could tear his eyes off of her, he looked around the kitchen. That didn't take long.

"What happened?"

"I don't know." I stood pressed hard up against the sink, and I had no plans to move.

"You been in there?" He jerked his head toward the living room.

I shook my head. He hesitated, started to say something, then, his hand on his gun, cautiously pushed open the swinging louvered door. I didn't miss him, for the kitchen rapidly filled up. Ambulance attendants, fireman, more policemen, all tried to fit into the tiny kitchen, most gaping at the body on the floor.

One policeman started pushing people out, yelling, "Get this place secured." He snarled at a volunteer fireman who seemed frozen in place, staring down at poor Dottie. "What's the matter with you? Haven't you ever seen a murder victim before?"

"No." The fireman's face was white under his

yellow helmet. He left the room a bit faster than he'd come in.

More people were coming up the driveway. Someone snapped a switch and the backyard was flooded with lights. Several people shouted at each other. It was a circus.

I was so absorbed watching the show that I jumped when I heard Gary's voice. "You the one that found her?"

I nodded again.

"When was that?" His hand still rested lightly on his gun.

"When I got here," I said, not very definitively. "As soon as I saw her, I dialed 911."

"But when?" he persisted. "What time? Why were you here this late?"

Something in his tone made me take a closer look at him. "She called me, and I came."

"Do you have a purse?"

"Of course I do," I replied. "I have several. I just don't seem to have one with me." I looked around. No purse. Had I left it in the car? Were my car keys there also? Who cared?

"Would you empty out your pockets, please?" Gary asked. He took a step back, or tried to. I watched him, confused. Purse? Pockets? Then I got it.

"Hey, wait a minute. You don't think— She was

lying there— I walked around— She didn't answer— I didn't do this!"

Alarm was giving way to indignation when Dan walked, or rather, squeezed in. He stared down at Dottie, his face impassive. Then caught sight of me. "What the hell are you doing here?"

"She called me, I came, then I found her, and now he— Oh, never mind."

"Never— What do you mean, she called you? I just left you! Why would she call you at this time of night?"

"There was a message on my machine. She sounded upset, so I came over. And it's not so late."

"It's too late to be gallivanting around town finding dead bodies. Why didn't you call me?"

"Because she wanted to talk to me. How was I supposed to know someone was going to kill her? And stop yelling."

"I'm not yelling." His teeth clenched, but he did lower his voice a little. "However, finding dead bodies is becoming a habit with you."

"It's not one I'm trying to develop." I said that as sourly as possible.

Dan and I glared at each other. "Come on." He grabbed me by the arm, stopped and turned to Gary. "You been in there?" He pointed to the swinging door.

"Yeah." Gary puffed his chest out a little. "No sign of anyone."

"Really." Dan's eyes bored holes in him. "Did you push the door open with your hand?"

Gary looked startled, then crestfallen. "Ah, I guess."

Dan sighed, pushed the door open using his shoulder and pulled me after him. We were in Dottie's small living room.

"Sit down there." He shoved me toward an old-fashioned rocker. "Don't move. Don't even think about it."

"What are you going to do?" I was still exasperated, but willing to get off my shaky legs.

"I'm going to see if I can salvage a crime scene." The bitterness in his voice did not bode well for some of the people milling aimlessly around in the kitchen. He stalked across the room toward the blaring TV and snapped it off. Noise from the front yard filled the room instead. He reached over and pulled the curtains aside. "What in God's name's going on out there?" He turned and ran out of the room.

Curious to see what had provoked such an interesting reaction, I got up, went to the window and pulled the curtains back. It was quite a spectacle. People were out of their houses, standing in little groups, blowing on their cold hands, stomping their slippered feet. Some wore clothes; most clutched their bathrobes tightly around them. A few actually ventured over Dottie's low fence and into the yard to get a better view. All seemed unwilling to go inside for fear they might miss something. The fire trucks completely filled the street, lights still flashed and there were a couple of new police cars. Uniformed people milled all over the garden area. No one was going to get convicted of this murder on the basis of footprints. I could see Dan yelling at people, clearing spectators and officers alike back from the house. Gradually something like order took shape.

"Sorry I startled you before." A voice sounded in my ear. I yelped, dropped the curtain and whirled around to find Gary earnestly peering at me. "I really didn't think— Well, we aren't used to murder around here, and, you know, you've been there both times. I— You all right?"

"Fine." I answered him as soon as my voice started working again. "Maybe I'll sit down." I headed back to Dottie's high-backed rocker and sank into it. Until Gary scared me, I hadn't realized how upset I was. I could feel myself start to shake, my stomach was doing odd things and I wanted desperately to cry. I was determined not to, especially with young Gary hovering over me.

"Are you all right?" he repeated.

I wanted to scream at him, *I just found the murdered body of a friend, it's the second dead body I've found in the last week, how do you think I am?* But before I could dissolve into hysterics, someone put their head through the swinging door and called out, "Gary, we need you."

"Leave that thing closed until I finish," a bald man in a baggy gray suit said, as Gary pushed through. I caught only a glimpse of him brushing something on the jamb before the door swung shut and I was alone.

I sat and rocked. I willed myself to be calm. I took deep breaths, closed my eyes and tried to empty my mind. Pretty soon I was calmer, but my eyes refused to stay closed, and my mind was crammed full of thoughts.

I started to feel restless. The sound of voices still came from the kitchen, but they seemed to be fewer, and more controlled. I wanted to know what was happening, but didn't feel up to risking Dan's wrath if I interrupted something. I looked around Dottie's small living room, really looked at it for the first time. A comfortable love seat covered in white, nubby material, strewn with pillows. A large easy chair, bright with big flowers, and a matching hassock. The rocking chair I was in, the TV, a bookshelf, a couple of low tables holding crystal lamps and a lovely, open, Chippendale-style slant-front desk completed the room. I got up and examined the books. Gardening books, books on antiques, some historical novels and a whole shelf of red-bound "classics." They didn't look used. I wandered over to the desk and absently looked at the things on it, but my ears strained to hear what was happening in the kitchen.

Gradually, the desk claimed my attention. It was so neat, so organized, just like Dottie. A pretty, flowered jug held pencils and pens, a shallow dish held paper clips. Opened bills were neatly stacked, ready to be paid. I wondered who would pay them now. Dottie had no family in Santa Louisa that I knew of. A lone envelope lay on the desk blotter. A Harper's Land Sales envelope. I took a closer look. It was addressed to Hank Sawyer.

I reached out to pick it up, but quickly drew back my hand. I had no idea what police procedure was for this kind of thing, or even if there was any. If I'd been alone, no police in the other room, then, maybe—but I wasn't, they were, and I figured I'd better get Dan.

I pushed at the door cautiously, peering through the crack. A man knelt beside Dottie, a stethoscope around his neck, putting away a long thermometer. "She was shot in the back, the bullet exited somewhere under her left breast. See?" He pointed down at Dottie. The blood had dried, and

I could see, for the first time, a shattered hole in the yellow sweatshirt. "She was dead when she hit the floor. Your guys find the bullet yet? Good." He stood up, grunted, made some notes in a book, then put everything in a black case.

"Send her over to the hospital. I'll do her in the morning." He nodded at Dan, who nodded back. He picked up his case and left.

Dan moved out of the way of a man with a flash camera, turned to say something to another man, who was carefully putting something in a brown paper bag, when he spotted me.

"I thought I told you to stay in there."

"You did, but I've found something."

"How could you find something if you'd stayed put?"

"For heaven's sake, Dan, I was only wandering around. Come in here."

Dan looked around the kitchen, seemed satisfied with what was going on, and followed me back into the living room.

I led him to the desk. "Look!"

"At what?"

"At the envelope, of course. It's addressed to Hank. I think you should open it."

"Why?"

I couldn't tell if Dan was deliberately acting dumb, or if he really thought whatever was in that envelope wasn't important. I stood, slightly open-mouthed, looking up at him, trying to think of something to say, but he saved me the trouble.

"Hey, Mike." That was addressed to the bald man who had just entered the living room. "You ready to start in here?"

"Yep." The man had powder, a paintbrush and what looked like clear tape ready, and was looking around, evidently for a good starting point.

"Do me a favor. Start here." Dan pointed at the desk.

The man shrugged and walked over toward us. Dan pulled me out of the way.

"What's he doing?"

"Fingerprinting."

"Why? If whoever shot Dottie was in here and saw that letter, he'd have taken it."

"Ellie." Dan ran his fingers through his hair. "First, we don't know that envelope has any connection to anything. Second, will you let me run my investigation my way?"

We did it his way.

Mike finished, and Dan finally reached for the letter. He gingerly opened the flap and slid out a sheet of paper. Names. It was nothing but names. Only this time there were two columns, and at the bottom, in Dottie's neat handwriting, was a note.

"Here is it, just like you asked. I hope you understand all this, because I don't."

"What does that mean?"

"I've no idea." He was studying the list, reading the names. Finally, he said, "This must be the new partners. Look, here's the Bullocks, Mary's friends, and here's Alice Ives. Beside them, and several of the others, are new names." He studied it some more. "It looks like James Robinson bought out the Bullocks and Paul Cameron took Alice's shares. Do you know any of these people?"

"Never heard of any of them. Do you suppose they're local?"

"Beats me. There's no addresses for them."

"Does it matter?"

"Don't know that either." He carefully folded the letter and put it back in the envelope. "I guess I'll hang on to this, but I'm not sure why. Let's see if they're through in the kitchen. If they are, you can go home."

"What are you going to do?" I didn't want to stay here, but I didn't want to go home either. Not alone. To an empty house.

"Oh, Ellie, my night's just starting," he said sadly. "Come on, let's see if we can get you out of here."

The kitchen was empty. Dottie was gone, leaving behind only a chalk mark on the kitchen floor.

The man with the paper sack was drawing diagrams in a notebook, and another man in a sports jacket and jeans stared at a hole in a cupboard door.

"Are you going to be all right?" Dan asked as I climbed into my car.

"I'll be fine," I assured him.

"Maybe I should call Mary, have her come over and spend the night." His hand was still on the car door.

The shakiness I'd had in the living room was back and threatening to get worse, but I wasn't going to let Dan know it.

"No," I said. "Don't do that. I'm all right. Really."

"You know, Ellie, a shock like this, you're bound to have a reaction. Even happens to us hardened police. Sure you don't want Mary?"

"I'm sure." I proved it with a weak smile.

"I'll call you in the morning." He watched me back slowly out of the driveway.

My knees held me up just long enough to close the garage door and make it into the kitchen. I collapsed in a straight-back chair and looked around. My nice, cozy, secure, safe house. I thought about Dottie. Why had someone killed her? She was a threat to someone, but who? I refused to believe Tom would kill her in cold blood. He might hit someone if he lost his temper, or even bash someone with a— I shuddered. Maybe. But shoot someone? In the back? I didn't believe it. Would Benjamin? He was crazy enough, but what could Dottie know about him? Ray, however, was a different story. Dottie and Hank had been seeing each other. Hank knew something incriminating about Ray and was going to expose him. Wasn't it likely Dottie also knew whatever it was? Maybe the evidence against Ray was in one of our office files. Dottie would know, and she'd know how to pull it out. I pictured Ray creeping around the side of Dottie's house, watching her through the window, easing open the kitchen door, waiting for her to turn her back, raising the gun…

Enough. I could feel cold sweat starting to break out. I got up, thinking, *I've got to go to bed. My flannel nightgown, and a small glass of brandy, that's what I need, and I'll be fine in the morning.* Then I did something I never do. I locked the back door.

TWENTY-TWO

MORNING ARRIVED, clear and brittle. The radio weatherman talked about record lows and the roof, lawn and fence posts were heavy with frost. Jake and I sat in my warm kitchen, staring out the window, me at nothing, Jake at whatever cats stare at. I was still in my bathrobe and slippers, working on my third cup of coffee and my fifteenth try at making sense of Dottie's death, when the phone rang.

"Hey, Mom." Susannah's voice rang out brightly in the gloom-laden atmosphere, and immediately I started to feel better.

"I thought I'd come up tomorrow afternoon, spend the weekend with you." She said that much too casually. "I thought you might need some company."

What she really meant was she wanted to do laundry, needed money or both. But it sounded great to me. "Honey, I can't think of anything I'd like better. Company is exactly what I need." Then I told her everything that had happened.

There was a loud silence from Susannah's end, then, "Are you all right?"

Bless the child. "Yes, I'm all right. Shook up, but all right."

"Well! It's a good thing I'm coming," she stated emphatically. "You don't need company. You need someone to run interference. I think you better stay in the house and keep the doors and windows locked until I get there."

Isn't youth wonderful? Susannah had reached the ripe old age of nineteen. I was over the hill at forty, and she was now going to take care of her aging mother.

"I'll see you tomorrow afternoon," I said, trying to keep the amusement out of my voice, "at which time I'll bring you up to date on unfolding developments."

"Be careful," instructed Susannah, "and don't forget to buy Oreos."

Life was back to normal. Almost. Anyway, moping was no longer an option. I put Jake outside, got myself into the shower and some clothes and headed for the office. I walked in on a major drama.

Dan was there, stern and official-looking. Young Gary, complete with notebook, was one step behind him. Tom, ashen faced, stood opposite them. Nicole pressed against Tom, her eyes wide and frightened. Sharon, poised in her office doorway, was the only one to look up as I entered.

"Tell me again," Dan said to Tom. "You were on Morning Glory Lane Sunday afternoon, but you didn't go into the house Hank was building, and you didn't see Hank. Is that right?"

Tom hesitated before answering. "Partly," he said finally. He glanced down at Nicole, then put his arm around her shoulders and pulled her closer into his side. "I was there, and I went into the house, but that was before Hank got there."

"Why?" Dan's blue eyes were as cold as steel and there was nothing friendly in that clipped single word.

"Because I didn't want to sell Hank's house, that's why." Tom's voice practically vibrated with bitterness. "I have a client who's interested in it. I hoped that other new one next door would work, and I could get them to buy it instead."

"And you never saw Hank?"

Tom hesitated again. He gave a shuddery little sigh that could have been a sob. "I saw him. I was in the next-door house and I watched him drive up. I didn't want to talk to him, so I waited until he got inside, then I left. I guess that's where I stepped in the drywaller's mud."

"And then what did you do?"

"I took them off. My shoes. They were just old

sneakers, ones Nicole'd been at me to throw out, and I knew that stuff would never come off."

"What did you do with them?" Dan looked pretty exasperated. I didn't blame him. Getting information out of Tom was as hard as getting pickles out of a jar.

"I threw them in the trunk, then drove to that new little store and bought running shoes. Ask the clerk. He'll remember."

"We'll ask. And the old shoes?"

"I threw them away." Nicole's voice was so faint I could barely hear it. "The trash man picked them up yesterday." Her voice got a little louder, and she moved a little straighter in Tom's arm. "And they didn't have any blood on them."

"That's going to be hard to prove, now they're gone." Dan's tone was mild, but his eyes weren't. "Tell me about Dottie."

"She saw me turning out of Morning Glory Lane." I didn't think it was possible for Tom to look more miserable, but he managed. "She asked me about it after Hank was found dead. I told her I'd seen Hank, but I didn't kill him. I didn't even speak to him. Dottie believed me."

"Did you see anyone else on that street?" Dan asked.

"No," Tom said. "All those houses are new, Hank's was the most finished. No one was around."

I started to ask Tom about Dottie's strange comment yesterday morning, took a good look at Dan's face and changed my mind.

"All right." Dan's patience was clearly on its last legs. "Dottie believed you. Why? What did she say?"

Tom looked down at Nicole, who nodded encouragement at him. "She said she knew I hadn't done it. She—well—she intimated she might know who had killed Hank, or at least why. She asked me not to say anything for a couple of days. I wanted to tell you, or someone, I'd been there, but Dottie was insistent. She said if I was a suspect the truth might never come out." Tom paused, then took a deep breath and went on. "I was scared, so I agreed."

That explained Dottie's comment yesterday. I was beginning to feel better. Surely Dan could see Tom was telling the truth, and that meant he'd look elsewhere. Benjamin? I hoped not. Ray? Sadly, that seemed only too possible.

"Have you told Chief Dunham about the gun in your glove compartment, Tom ol' boy?"

I gave an involuntary little gasp and whirled around. I hadn't heard Ray come in, but there he was, smiling, but there was no mirth in it. He couldn't have announced his arrival more dramatically if he'd dropped a bomb, which I guess he did. Tom stiffened, Nicole moaned, Sharon muttered something under her breath. Unfortunately, Dan looked interested.

"A gun? A little something you forgot to mention?" There was a hint of sarcasm in his voice as he studied Tom. "Maybe you'd like to give me a look."

"He has a permit." Nicole's chin went up and she stood a little straighter.

"I'm sure he does." Dan's expression didn't get any friendlier. "I'd still like a look. And while we're getting it, why don't you tell me where you were last night between, oh, let's say nine and ten."

"He was home with me. All night." Even I could tell she was lying.

"Oh, but…" It was the first thing Sharon had said. She clamped her mouth shut like she was sorry she'd let that much escape.

"But what, Sharon?" Dan looked over at her and it was obvious he expected an answer.

She flushed a little, glanced at Tom, and quickly looked away. "I thought I saw Tom going into the AM PM about nine-thirty. Maybe I was wrong."

"Was she?" Dan looked Tom, who shook his head.

"No, she's right. I ran out for milk, but I wasn't

gone long. And I'd hardly have stopped off to shop if I'd just come from shooting Dottie, now, would I?"

"Sounds like a great alibi to me," Ray said nastily.

Dan glared at him and Ray backed up a step. "I don't know what you might do," Dan said, "but I'd like to see that gun. Let's go."

He gestured toward the office door. Tom, Nicole still crunched against his side, headed out onto the street, all of us close behind.

Tom opened the unlocked door of his Jeep Cherokee, slid in, snapped up the lid of the center storage box and fumbled around inside. The fumbling became more frantic. He looked up at Dan and said numbly, "It's not here."

"Look in the glove box." Nicole's voice was shrill, on the edge of panic.

Tom pulled everything out of both places, dumping it all on the seats. No gun. He sat on the edge of the seat, disbelief written all over his face. "It's gone, the gun is gone," he kept repeating. "It's gone."

Dan had bent over, watching Tom's frantic search. Now he straightened up and tapped the distraught Tom on the shoulder. "I think we need to continue this conversation at the station."

Nicole made a small mewing sound. Tom said faintly, "Am I under arrest?"

"You'll know it when you are." Dan reached over and took him by the arm. "Right now, we're going to talk. Come on."

Sharon and I were left standing on the sidewalk, looking helplessly after their retreating backs. I looked around for Ray, wondering why he hadn't come out to the car to watch the futile search.

The front door opened and Ray came out, carrying his briefcase and examining his watch.

"I have a listing appointment." Self-righteousness oozed from every syllable as he brushed past us.

"How did you know Tom had a gun?" I inserted myself in front of him as he tried to go around me.

He paused and gave me one of his best condescending looks. "He told me." He sidestepped, clicked the remote that unlocked his Lincoln, climbed in and roared away.

I felt like throwing rocks at him. My suspicion that he might be our murderer deepened, or maybe I just kept hoping. I turned to Sharon, expecting her to feel as angry as I did, but instead she looked crushed, like old parchment ready to crumble if touched.

"Oh, are you all right?"

"No." Even her voice seemed ready to crumble. "I'm going inside, having a huge cup of coffee and not answering the phone. At least for a few minutes."

I followed her through the door, watched her collapse into the chair behind her desk, poured us both very full cups of vile-smelling coffee and let myself down into the chair opposite her.

"What do you think?" Sharon's hand trembled a little on the handle of her cup, which she hadn't even tried to lift.

"Do I think Tom killed Dottie? Or Hank?" I shook my head. "No, I don't. Do I think Dan has a case against him? It's beginning to look like it."

"So you think Tom is innocent?" She finally sipped from her coffee cup. It must have done her some good, awful as it was, for color was returning to her face.

"I know it looks bad. He and Hank fought, Tom admits being on Morning Glory Lane about the time Hank was killed, his fingerprints are on the closet door, you saw him out last night about the time Dottie was killed, but, even if he lost his temper and hit Hank, he'd never shoot Dottie in the back."

"Hum." Sharon sat up a little straighter, absently readjusted the heavy gold necklace she wore over an ivory silk sweater. "If not Tom, who?" She watched me carefully, as if sure I had the answer.

"I don't know." I sighed. "I'd love it to be someone we never heard of, but that's not possible. Benjamin? Only I can't think why he'd kill Dottie." I hesitated before I rushed on. "Ray seems possible."

"Ray?" Sharon had been about to take another swallow but set her cup back down on her desk instead. Probably it was an excuse not to drink the awful stuff. "Why Ray?"

"He seems the most logical." I was surprised she hadn't already thought this through. "Hank evidently had some kind of evidence that might get Ray's license removed. Dottie must have known what that was, and where to find it. Both Hank and Dottie are dead. It's impossible not to think of Ray."

"I see what you mean." Sharon spoke slowly, as if trying to work it all out. "Only, Tom has the gun."

"Not anymore. It's gone." I was following a new thought trail. "I'll bet the police tear Tom and Nicole's place apart looking for it, but it won't be there."

"What are you saying, Ellen? That someone took Tom's gun?" She picked up the cup, looked in it, grimaced and set it back down.

"It's possible." I warmed to my subject as I spoke. "Tom never locks his car. Anybody who knew it was there could have taken it. You—me—

anybody. Ray certainly knew about it." Another thought struck me. "Did Benjamin know about the gun?"

"I've no idea." Sharon dismissed Benjamin and went on with her own thoughts. "Do you know who Dottie suspected of killing Hank?"

"No. She never said anything. But she left a message for me to come over to her place last night. She said she had something she wanted to talk about. I did, and that's when I found her."

"She wanted to talk to you? About what?" Sharon looked a little apprehensive, as well she might. One of her agents was practically under arrest for murder, another certainly should be under suspicion, her secretary was dead, as well as her best client. I wouldn't be apprehensive, I'd be darn near crazy.

"She didn't say, but it may have had something to do with that list she left for Hank."

"We already talked about the list. What was there for her to say?"

"This was a different list. It had all the old partners names, then beside some of them, new names. I guess the new partners. Paul Cameron, I remember that one. Is he a new partner?"

"Yes," Sharon said slowly, "but I don't understand. What would Dottie want with that?"

"I've no idea, but the list was in an envelope

addressed to Hank. Evidently he wanted it for something."

"I can't imagine what." Sharon put her hand up to her head and rubbed her temple. She looked around her office, at the stacked files, the pile of message slips, the silent phone. "My head is splitting, and when that blasted phone rings, it won't be about real estate. It's going to be either the press or curious clients. I can't take either right now." She stood up, pushed several of the files into her briefcase and closed it. "I'm going home and taking several aspirin, but no more coffee." She looked at her still half-filled cup and shuddered. "You can stay here if you want. Ray will be back soon. He'll help you if something comes up you can't handle. Or put the phones on answering service, whatever you want."

She left me staring after her, wondering what I should do. The thought of being alone with Ray gave me the creeps, but I somehow felt guilty leaving the office. Besides, where would I go? I started to rub my own temples, wondering if headaches were catching and if Tylenol could cure depression.

The front door opened. I could hear it but couldn't see who it was from my chair in Sharon's small office. What if it was Ray? How could I get by without him doing—what? Fear, unreasonable fear, held me rigid. I strained to hear, wondering if I should make a dive for the phone.

"Is anyone here?"

The voice sounded familiar and very female. I stood up and took a tentative step out into the office. Pat Bennington stared down at Dottie's empty desk.

"Oh, Ellen," she gasped. "You scared me. It's so quiet in here."

"You scared me, too." I found I had to blink back tears. "I'm turning into a nervous wreck."

"It's true, then?" Pat spoke softly, her gaze returning once more to the desk. "Someone shot Dottie Fielding in the back last night?"

"Yes." I felt the return of the sorrow that had engulfed me earlier that morning. "I found her."

"Dear God, Ellen. How horrible."

Pat's sympathy was not good for my control. Blinking wasn't going to keep those tears in check much longer.

"Who could have done such a thing?" she went on. "Dottie was so— Well, she was hardly— Dottie was sweet."

"She was," I agreed, sniffing a little, "but she must have known something about someone."

Pat examined my face, reached into her pocket and handed me a slightly rumpled tissue. "You look like you need some caffeine therapy. Let's go to the Yum Yum and get some coffee. You can tell me everything there."

I already had caffeine surging through every vein, but a good dose of practical, sympathetic Pat was what I needed to take the edge off my jitters.

"Let me call the service and lock up." I reached for my keys. Too late. The phone rang.

"Aren't you going to answer?" Pat asked me as I stared down at it in dismay. I sighed and picked it up. It was a Mr. Leon Marburger from Stop N Shop, wanting Sharon.

"I talked with her a couple of weeks ago, telling her I'd be in town for a meeting. I'll be available tomorrow and would like to see some of the homes she told me about. Would it be possible to make an appointment? I realize our arrangement was somewhat vague, but I really would like to get an idea—you know?"

I didn't know, but wasn't about to tell him that. Instead, I made a tentative appointment for the morning, said I'd have Sharon confirm as soon as possible, scribbled a note for Ray, grabbed Pat and fled.

Ruthie loped over the minute she spotted us, perennial coffeepot in hand. Barely acknowledging Pat, she was all over me.

"Oh, Ellen. We've all just heard. What a time you've had! I can't believe what's goin' on in this town, and here you are, caught slap-dab in the middle." She waved the pot in our faces. "And Dottie Fielding, of all people. Who'd want to hurt poor Dottie?" There was no answer to that question. Pat and I sat down at an empty table without even trying to provide one. I couldn't believe Ruthie. I'd met her one time and here she was acting like we were sisters or something. I thought for a moment she was going to hug me, so I kept a close eye on that bobbing pot. Luckily, she used it to fill our cups, then, promising to be right back, trotted off to tend to the needs of other pre-lunch customers.

The buzz of conversation seemed to have fallen off while we were seating ourselves but picked back up. I glanced around. The stares I'd felt seemed to fade away. I looked back at Pat who was sipping her coffee.

"Yes, they're all talking about you." She didn't try to hide a smile. "After all, Ellen, you can't be gone for years, return a jaded divorcee, find two dead bodies, get romantically linked with the police chief and not get talked about. Not in this town, anyway."

Jaded? Me? What romance?

"What are you talking about?" I was alarmed and a more than a little irritated. "Even in this town women must get divorced, especially if they're landed with a philandering egotist like Dr. Brian McKenzie. And I'll happily let anyone who wishes find the next dead body."

Pat grimaced. "Let's hope there's not another one to find. Besides, it's your romantic link to Dan Dunham that's making headline news."

"What romantic link?" I was getting more indignant by the minute. "Dan and I grew up next door to each other, we were best friends. We're still friends, nothing more." I looked around the small room, ready to stare down anyone who looked my way.

"Small town, Ellen. You can't stop gossip, especially in this case. Nothing this gruesome has ever happened that I can remember, and everyone has a theory. The only thing they all agree on is you're right in the middle. Some have you in grave danger because you know something, others think you were in the wrong place at the wrong time, and a few hint darkly that finding two dead bodies is too much of a coincidence." Pat smiled broadly at the horrified expression on my face before she went on. "No matter which of the above theories people subscribe to, most have you and Dan halfway down the church aisle. I've even heard a rumor regarding a reception menu."

"You are kidding." I choked down a mouthful of coffee before I could get words out. "Aren't you?"

I felt like someone had opened a valve and all my wind had rushed out. "People actually think I may be the murderer? Or that Dan and I might— Not seriously."

"Don't let it get to you, Ellen. No one really thinks you killed anyone, and most of the married women have been trying to get Dan remarried since he came back to town. The single ones, well, a few of them have taken up that project as well. So far, no one's been very successful. Remember, this is a small town. Tongues will wag. Sometimes pleasantly, sometimes not."

Before I could say anything, Ruthie was back, setting a bowl of soup down in front of each of us.

"Ellen, I'll bet you haven't eaten a thing all day and that's a surefire way to get sick."

At least she doesn't think I'm a mass murderer, I thought as I looked down at the soup. I was so upset I was sure I couldn't swallow a mouthful, but the aroma of broccoli and cheese met my empty stomach, reminding me that all I'd had for breakfast was coffee. Lots of coffee. Ruthie was right. It would be a shame to get sick.

"I'm going to take my break now, before this place fills up." Ruthie pulled over a chair, set the coffeepot in the middle of the table and produced a mug from somewhere.

"Is what we're hearin' really true, Ellen? Dottie was shot, in her very own kitchen?"

Ruthie made it sound like Dottie dying in her kitchen was the worst indignity of all. I couldn't answer, my mouth was full, but I nodded.

Ruthie's voice got a little shrill. "What's happening in this town? We got some kind of maniac loose?" She looked imploringly at Pat, as though for reassurance, then back at me.

"What does Dan think?" Pat asked. "Does he have any ideas?"

"Dan's got ideas, all right," I answered with maybe a trace of anger as I finished the last spoonful of soup and pushed the empty bowl away. "The trouble is, they're all wrong."

"What do you mean?" Pat had barely touched her own soup. "Does he think he knows who killed Dottie? Is it the same person who killed Hank? Is it someone we know?" There was dread in her voice.

"He took Tom Chambers in for questioning."

Shock and dismay showed clearly in both faces.

"No," Ruthie finally said. "Dan can't think Tom would do such a thing. Why, that boy grew up in this town. We've known him since he was a baby. No way it's him." Ruthie's voice got more agitated as she spoke. She'd picked up the coffeepot to refill our cups and now waved it over the table. I was afraid we were all about to be baptized.

Pat reached over and rescued the pot, and us. "Why? Why Tom? I can't believe he'd harm Dottie. Especially like that." She had a sick look on her face.

"What kind of harebrained reason does Dan Dunham have for suspecting him, anyway?" demanded Ruthie.

"I'll tell you the whole story." I did, ending with the missing gun.

Neither of them said anything for a moment. Ruthie pushed back her chair, picked up the coffeepot, turned and walked away. She said something I couldn't quite hear, but it sounded a lot like "shit."

We silently watched her go. Pat looked down at her watch, sighed and said, almost apologetically, "I've got to go. I work part-time in my husband's office and I'm due there now. Look, all we're doing going over and over this is giving ourselves ulcers. We're going to have to trust the police to come up with the right answers, no matter how much we don't like them."

She got up, paused and went on. "Are you coming to The Little Theater meeting tomorrow night? At least it will give you something new to think about. Lord knows you could use some distracting about now, and let me assure you, some of our members are very distracting."

She laughed a little ruefully. I laughed also, and agreed to come. Pat said she'd call me, left some change on the table and hurried out. I sat for another moment, finished my coffee, and took another look around. Tables were rapidly filling. The lunch hour had begun.

Suddenly I felt lost. I didn't want to go back to the office. I wasn't in the mood to take messages, and I didn't want to answer anyone's questions about Hank or Dottie. I especially didn't want to be alone with Ray. The thought of shopping made me shudder, especially as the Emporium was the only choice. The library, my old refuge? No. Not today. I was much too restless to concentrate on a book. So, I decided to do what any sensible woman would do. I'd go home, change into my jeans and prepare my sadly overdue sweet pea bed.

I was changed and ready to find my shovel when I thought of Aunt Mary. I hadn't called her. She was bound to be upset about Dottie, and even more that she hadn't heard from me.

The phone rang several times. I was beginning to get worried when she picked it up.

"You sound out of breath. What are you doing?"

"Pruning the rose bushes. Attacking something

with the loppers seemed like a good idea. Are you all right?"

The last thing those rose bushes needed was any more pruning, but I understood her feeling. "Depressed, upset, scared but hanging in there." I brought her up to date on everything that had happened last night and this morning. Naturally, she knew most of it.

"You know, Ellen," she said when I was finished, "the worst part is that the murderer has to be someone we know. There was some link between Dottie and Hank, and I don't for one minute believe it was sex. When we understand that link, we'll know who's responsible for all this."

"Then you still don't think it was Tom, in spite of all Dan's evidence?"

She snorted. "Of course not. Do you?"

"No," I said slowly, "I don't, and I'm not convinced Dan does either. You're right, though, about Hank and Dottie."

"Dan needs to look harder at what was going on between them. You tell him I said so."

Why did she assume I'd see Dan before she would, I wondered, as I headed for the backyard. I probably wouldn't see him for days. My mind filled with thoughts of Ray as I turned over dirt. He had a motive for both deaths. At least, it seemed he might if Hank really had some kind of evidence that could put Ray's license at risk. Then there was Benjamin. I thought about him as I dragged fertilizer sacks out of the garage. He had the best reason to kill Hank. Protecting his store was a huge motive, but how did Dottie fit in? Could Benjamin be trying to sabotage the partnership that Sharon put together? If Stop N Shop couldn't buy the land, they couldn't come. Benjamin had been pretty sure that with Hank dead the store wouldn't be built, and he'd been bothered by Dottie's comments at the Sawyer house. How did that fit? I thought of ways while jabbing seeds into the ground. Could Benjamin be talking to the old partners, or the new ones, giving them false information of some kind, trying to talk them into not selling right away? Maybe Hank and Dottie suspected, and were trying to stop him.

I absently covered over the last of the seeds and stood up, my mind still on Benjamin, when the phone rang. I ran for the house, wiping my muddy hands on my jeans. It was Dan.

"What are you doing?"

"Playing in the mud."

There was a brief silence. "What?"

"Never mind. Why?"

"I thought I'd take you to dinner. If, of course, you aren't already doing something."

"No, I'm not. And I could use some company."

I sighed. "I don't want to get dressed up. How do you feel about takeout Chinese?"

"This is Santa Louisa. No one gets dressed up. But I like it. Do you have wine, or shall I bring some?"

I laughed. "I have some. Bring tea bags and egg rolls. I'll lay the fire, but you have to poke it."

"It's a deal," Dan said. "See you about six-thirty, little white cartons in hand."

I found myself humming as I headed for the bathroom to shower and change. Before I could get out of the kitchen, the phone rang again. This time it was Alice Ives.

"Ellen, dear, I wondered if tomorrow would be a good time for you to come over. I do think we should get started on whatever it is you people do. I'm sure it must be very complicated and…"

Alice, of course. My first listing appointment and I'd forgotten all about her. The fact that the events of the last few days had been somewhat distracting was no excuse. It took me a few minutes to stem the tide, but I finally did, and we settled on two o'clock the next afternoon. Then Alice said, "I heard about Dottie Fielding. That was the most terrible thing. Mildred told me you found her. That's not true, is it, dear? Oh, how horrible for you. Now that I think of it, there will be a service, won't there, and I think Mildred said

Saturday morning. You'll want to go, and I will, too, so maybe…"

I had no choice but to interrupt her again. "Alice, how about Sunday, early afternoon. One o'clock? I'll have everything with me, and we'll get it done then."

Hearing what I took for agreement, I firmly ended the conversation and hung up, smiling and feeling a little breathless. I wondered if Alice had that effect on everyone. I started upstairs again, but Alice's call reminded me. Real estate. Sharon. Mr. Marburger and their appointment. Had the answering service reached her? I turned back into the kitchen and dialed her number. It rang and rang. No answer, no machine. I shrugged and headed upstairs. This time I made the shower, and just in time. My hair was barely dry when the back door opened and a voice yelled out, "Where are you?"

TWENTY-THREE

WONDERFUL SMELLS WAFTED from the big brown bag Dan placed on the chopping block. He was rummaging in a drawer, a bottle of local sauvignon blanc in his hand.

"If you're looking for an opener, that's the wrong drawer." I pointed to the correct one. He grinned at me, found the opener, expertly removed the cork and took two glasses down from the rack.

"Hi. You look kind of damp."

I sighed. That's exactly what he would have said when he was twelve and I was ten. But then, that's the kind of friendship we had. Wasn't it?

"Might rain." Dan handed me a glass. "Clouds are coming in and it's not nearly so cold. Hey, get off there." He picked up Jake, who had been investigating the possibilities of the brown sack, and set him on the floor. Jake walked off, legs stiff, whiskers quivering, toward the living room, pretending neither of us existed.

I laughed. "You ruffled his dignity. You'll have to give him your shrimp or he won't forgive you."

"He gets leftovers." Dan opened cupboards until

he found the ones with the plates. "How did you know I got shrimp? Where do you keep the napkins?"

"You always got shrimp. You were the only kid on the block who liked it. The napkins are right behind you."

Dan pulled white cartons from the sack, rummaged through my silverware drawer, came up with two large serving spoons and started dishing food out onto plates. He stole a look at me and smiled. "So you remembered that?"

I nodded and smiled back

"You know, Ellie, this place looks the same, yet different. Your doing? Pot stickers?"

"Yes," I said. "To both. Mother took all her things with her to Scottsdale, which was fine with me. I moved my stuff in, and everything took on a whole different look. I still have a lot packed away, I haven't really made up my mind what I'm going to do, but I hate living out of boxes, so…" I waved my hand at the kitchen. It did look nice. So did the living room. The only things I had purchased were the crisp white tie-backs on the kitchen windows. Everything else I had brought from my life in Southern California. For some reason, all my possessions seemed much more at home in this old house.

"I thought you were buying this house from

your folks. I didn't realize you might not stay here.
Where would you go?" He handed me a full plate,
juggled his own along with his glass and the wine
bottle and started for the living room. He set everything down on the coffee table, looked meaningfully at the fireplace, which didn't contain a
fire, then started filling it with wood. I sat on the
sofa, sipped my wine and watched him. He had it
roaring before I answered him.

"I don't know that I'll go anywhere. Maybe I'll
love it here, love selling real estate and never want
to leave." I was feeling so peaceful, the fire, wine,
Chinese food, my old friend Dan, I couldn't imagine wanting to be anyplace else. Yet, you never
know. "I made a deal with my folks to rent this
house for a year. Then we'll see if they like Scottsdale, and if I like living here."

Dan looked at me with an unreadable expression. "You're probably right. You shouldn't take
change too fast."

I wasn't sure how to respond, so instead I asked,
"Where do you live?"

"I'm renting a condo out by the golf course."

"For some reason, I see you owning an old
house around here someplace."

"I guess I didn't want to make that kind of com-
mitment, it was too soon. But lately, I've been
thinking about it."

"Oh." I wondered where the conversation was headed. I finished the last of my fried rice, keeping out a bite of pork. "Are you going to give that little bit of shrimp to Jake?"

He laughed. "If I want to get back in his good graces, I guess I'd better. Will he come down for my whistle?"

The cat sat on his favorite bookshelf, pretending not to watch us eat. Dan whistled. Jake sailed down on the back of the sofa on his way to the coffee table.

"No. Not off my plates. In his bowl."

I gathered up the empty plates and glasses, Dan picked up Jake and we all headed for the kitchen. "Tea?"

Dan filled Jake's bowl and put it on the floor. "Sounds great. I haven't had such a relaxed night in ages, including last night. The first part, that is."

I made a face at him as I got out cups. "Of all the places you could have gone, why here? Your family moved away ages ago."

He leaned against the kitchen door, watching me. Except for the mustache and the light frosting of gray at his temples, he looked for all the world like the boy I had grown up with. Fleetingly, I wondered how much I still looked like the girl he remembered.

"I needed to get out of San Francisco. The job

of Chief came up here, the town offered it to me and I took it. I took a pay cut, too." He gave a rueful little laugh, and shook his head.

"Are you glad you came back?"

"I was until this week. Now, I'm not so sure. Violence, murder, you don't see much of that in a town like this, which was a big reason I came." His smile faded, his eyes looked tired and somehow sad. "Now, I'm back chasing a murderer, and this time I'm going to end up arresting someone I know. Possibly a friend." He grinned again. "Your coming home has been the only bright spot in an otherwise miserable week."

The conversation was doubling back on itself. "How's that fire doing?"

"I don't know." That faint smile he kept getting was playing under his mustache. "Why don't we go in the living room and find out?"

Dan sat on the sofa; I sat in my big reading chair. Jake curled up on Dan's lap.

"Dan." I decided to be blunt. "Did you arrest Tom?"

"No, not yet." He held his cup away from Jake's exploring paw. "It's hot," he told the cat, "and it's drinkable, not edible."

"Why?" I sat curled up in the chair, as relaxed as Dan. He was right. The last few days had been about as stressful as anything I'd been through, including leaving Brian. So why was I pursuing the subject? Because I might be working with a murderer, that was why. And that fact was pretty stressful as well. "Are you having doubts he's guilty, or don't you have enough evidence?"

"Both." Dan gave up, put the cat on the floor and his cup on the table. "The case against him has holes big enough to drive a truck through, but still, everything we come up with points his way. We're not through digging."

"How about Vera?"

"You know better," was the reply I expected.

"Well then, what about Benjamin Lockwood?"

"Why Benjamin?" The teasing look was back in Dan's eyes, but something more. Interest? In Benjamin?

"Because he has a stronger motive than Tom's. If Stop N Shop is built, Benjamin is convinced he'll be out of business."

"His business may not last long enough for the new store to break ground."

"Having had the privilege of shopping there, I agree. Nevertheless, Benjamin's blaming it for all his woes, and he blamed Hank for supporting it."

"All right." Dan sat back down. Jake immediately returned to his lap. He started to stroke Jake's ears, but he didn't relax back on the sofa and he frowned as he carefully chose his words. "If it was only Hank, I could buy into that theory, but how do you tie in Dottie? Old Ben just doesn't have a motive."

"I've been thinking." Dan groaned. I threw a pillow at him, he started to throw it back, but Jake reached up and batted it. Dan laughed, and tossed it on the end of the sofa instead.

"All right, Ellie. Tell me why Benjamin Lockwood might want to kill Dottie Fielding."

"I thought it all out while I planted sweet peas." I had to stop until Dan had quit whooping. What was so funny about sweet peas, I didn't know. "Suppose somehow Benjamin knew who all the partners were in that land thing of Sharon's. Suppose he made up a story about another store wanting to buy the land, one that would pay more money but wouldn't come for, oh, another couple of years, and was trying to convince everyone to make Sharon wait. Suppose Hank and Dottie found out, or suspected something, and he killed them both to keep them quiet."

"*Suppose* is a good word," Dan said wryly. "I don't suppose you have any proof?"

"No, not exactly, but something like that could be true."

"I'm afraid the police can't operate on what could be. We need facts." Dan moved Jake from one knee to the other. "There isn't one fact to connect Benjamin with any of this."

The man wanted facts? I silently vowed to find some. Benjamin was just fanatical enough to think killing Stop N Shop's chances, along with Hank and Dottie, would save his dying store, and if he was guilty, I was going to find that first "fact" to start Dan looking Benjamin's way.

"Benjamin tried to take Hank's seat on the Planning Commission. That's a fact."

"A fact of political intrigue and he lost." Dan's voice was mild. The cat rolled over and he started to scratch his belly. I could hear Jake's loud purr of contentment loud and clear. "It has nothing to do with murder. Anyway, I thought Ray Yarbourough was your choice for chief suspect."

"How did you know…"

"I'm afraid Ray's rather obvious." Dan quit scratching. Jake took his paw and tried to pull Dan's hand back onto his belly. It worked. "Hank's accusations, Dottie's access to all Ray's real estate files, it makes Ray a little hard to overlook."

"Then why haven't you arrested him?"

"Same reason we haven't arrested Tom." Dan removed his hand, avoided Jake's paw and set him on the pillow I'd thrown at him. "I need evidence." He stood up, stretched and yawned. "I'm going home and hitting the bed. I only had two hours' sleep last night. I hope to God this town stays quiet. Promise me something."

"What?"

"No matter what happens, no matter who calls, you won't leave this house tonight. At least, not without calling me first."

We had made it to the front door. I looked up at him in exasperation. "Really, Dan..." I started. He interrupted me by putting his finger under my chin and lifting up my face.

"Promise." He hesitated, as though making up his mind, then bent down and gave me a feather-light kiss on the lips. I was so shocked I couldn't think of a thing to say. He could. "And, Ellie, don't forget to lock the door." He walked out and closed it gently behind him.

Well, I thought. *Well, of all the nerve!* I gave the door a kick. "Ahhh." I danced around the living room holding my big toe. Jake rushed upstairs to the safety of the bed. I glared after him, then at the dying fire, the empty cups, the empty room. Why had he done that? We were friends. Old friends, nothing more. Kisses, no matter how light, were for...friends. I limped into the kitchen, berating myself for letting all the bad emotions Brian left me with spill over onto Dan. My good friend Dan.

It was still early but I hadn't slept much last night either. *My soft flannel nightgown, my book and another cup of tea, that's what I need,* I thought, as I stacked the last of the dishes in the washer. I wouldn't think about murder, my new job, my new life, ruined marriages or old friendships. I'd give myself up to the comforts of a warm bed, with only Jake for company.

TWENTY-FOUR

IT WAS COLD. If we'd had any rain it had finished early, because the temperature had taken another nosedive. I lay with the covers pulled tightly up around me, Jake firmly curled at my side, thinking how nice it was I didn't have to move. At least, not for a while. I hoped the automatic coffeepot had done its job. Warm, drowsy, I went over the events of the night before. Dan, Chinese food, that had been fun. He'd kissed me. But a grown-up, friendly kiss, nothing more. There was something about it, though—

I had no intention of going on with that thought. Besides, it was past time I was up and moving. Pushing Jake aside, I found my robe and slippers and headed downstairs.

The wonderful aroma of fresh coffee met me. I poured a mug and stood at the kitchen window, wondering if wool slacks, a sweater and boots could substitute for a skirt. Sharon would be in a dress, or suit, she always was, but that didn't mean... Sharon. Had she gotten her message about Mr. Marburger? I picked up the phone and dialed.

No answer. She hadn't called the service for messages either. Damn! Now what?

I took another swallow of coffee and thought. It didn't seem like efficient, dedicated Sharon not to pick up messages, but the stress of the last few days was enough to break anyone. The question now wasn't where Sharon was, but what I did about Mr. Marburger. I couldn't ignore him, but I did not want to take that appointment myself. Call Tom or Nicole? Out of the question. Ray? Yes, Ray! No, not Ray. He'd been talking all week about a big listing appointment he had this morning, and I knew he'd never cancel it for one of Sharon's clients.

That left only me. So, muttering under my breath, I headed for the shower.

I was putting out a reluctant Jake when the phone rang. Praying it was Sharon, I ran back inside to answer it. It was Susannah.

"Hey, Mom. I thought I'd better make sure you're all right. You are, aren't you?"

"I'm fine." I was immediately alarmed. "Is something wrong? Aren't you coming?"

"Of course I'm coming. By the way, are you stopping at the store?"

A few minutes later, Susannah's grocery list stuffed in my purse, I was on my way to the office. It had a bleak, abandoned look. Dottie's empty desk was an ever-present reminder of the past week's terrible events. No time to think about that now. I ran around picking up maps of the town, propaganda put out by the Chamber of Commerce and various other groups, arranged it neatly in a folder, then tried to decide on a couple of homes to show this man. I had no idea what he expected, and my first try at showing homes hadn't been too successful. Exciting, though. I hoped this time it would be a lot duller. Ready as I'd ever be, I picked up my briefcase, locked the office once more and headed for City Hall where I was to pick up Mr. Marburger.

I pushed open the glass doors of our antique City Hall and looked around. Mr. Marburger was in with the city planners. I was to meet him outside the conference room door. Only, I had no idea where that was.

A frosted glass window that stated it had Information was right in front of me. I walked up to it and slid my card toward the woman behind the counter. She had huge brown eyes, a pleasant smile and a vaguely familiar look. She glanced down at my card, back up at me uncertainly, as if she should know me.

"I'm looking for the Planning conference room. I'm to meet Mr. Marburger, from Stop N Shop."

"They're all in that room right down there." She pointed at closed double doors about halfway down the hall, looked at my card once more, then her face lit up. "Of course. Page. You're Ellen Page. You remember me, don't you? Juanita…"

I didn't hear the rest as the conference room doors opened and people started pouring out. Mr. Marburger wasn't hard to identify. Perfectly tailored three-piece suit, silk tie, highly polished wing tips, not the usual attire seen on our streets. Past middle age, slightly overweight but not flabby, brisk, confident stride, he gave off an air of boardrooms and corporate structure.

I waved in the general direction of Juanita, who smiled and nodded at me. Accepting the inevitable, I walked up to Mr. Marburger and thrust out my hand.

He looked at me blankly for a second before he took it. "Yes," he said, a faint question in his voice.

"I'm Ellen McKenzie, Sharon Harper's associate. She was called away and asked me to fill in for her this morning."

"Oh." He looked at me more closely. "Well, fine. Let me put this briefcase in the car, and we'll get started."

He settled himself in the passenger seat of my car and looked at me expectantly. "I'm sure Sharon told you what I am looking for. This is just a preliminary to bringing my wife here, so I won't take up too much of your time."

"Actually—" I tried to sound professional and confident, but it wasn't working out too well "—this all came up so fast, Sharon didn't have a chance to tell me much, so…"

"Oh. Well, then." He looked a little dubious. "You know that our company has been dealing with Sharon on the purchase of land for one of our stores?"

I nodded. He seemed somewhat relieved.

"I've been impressed by your town on my visits here," he went on, "and, since I will be retiring soon, this seemed like a good place to relocate. If I—we—can find a place we like, we'll use it for weekends until we move here permanently."

He looked at me as if that explained everything. It didn't. However, I couldn't sit there, so I handed him the folder of information I'd gathered. "I thought you'd like some information on the town, its history and everything." I started the engine with no clear idea where we were headed.

"Yes." He barely glanced at it. "We have quite a lot of information from Sharon, but I'll take this to my wife. I hope you're going to show me something in your hills. We'd like something with a view, but still in town. We're used to a large house, but this one can be a little smaller, not too much land, but privacy, of course."

That eliminated every house I had planned to

show him. I started for the west side of town, frantically searching my memory for anything that might fit. One mercifully came to mind. It was vacant and had a view. At least, it was a place to start.

Mr. Marburger proved to be quite chatty. Most of his conversation was about the virtues of Sharon.

"A very efficient little lady. Yes, sir. She's kept this whole deal on track right from the beginning. Why, when she first approached us a couple of years ago, I would have said we'd never get this done, and here we are, almost ready to close."

"I didn't realize this had been going on so long. Somehow I thought you'd only been negotiating a few months." I wasn't really listening. Where was that house? I couldn't remember, and was starting to panic.

"Oh, no." Mr. Marburger chuckled gently at my naivety. "These things take time, lots of it."

"I've only been back in town a few weeks." I hoped that would serve as an excuse for my obvious ignorance. But I'd found the house.

Mr. Marburger politely, but firmly, let me know he hated it. This whole thing was turning out to be a fiasco. Mr. Marburger wanted to see more houses. I desperately wanted to go home. I found three more houses, which he didn't like any better, and finally, after what seemed like days, delivered him back to City Hall.

"Now, Ellen," he said, in what I'm sure he thought was a kindly voice, "don't feel bad. You know what I want now, and next time I'm in town, we'll look again. It takes a while for someone to become as good as Sharon, you know. Don't be discouraged."

I didn't know it showed. Besides, it wasn't discouragement I felt. It was rage. At Mr. Marburger for being nice, and Sharon Harper for putting me in an impossible position.

Mr. Marburger drove off, and I went back to the office to pick up messages. There weren't any. Neither was there any sign of Sharon. It was lunchtime, and I decided I was starved. Eating alone held no appeal, so I dialed the police station, looking for Dan. A bored voice told me he wasn't in, didn't know where he was or when he was expected. The implication was strong it was none of my business. I sat at my desk, trying to decide what to do, when I spotted a piece of paper I hadn't noticed before. I glanced at it, and then picked it up. It was information on the house Sharon had listed Sunday afternoon. As I read it, I became more and more excited. This was Mr. Marburger's house, I was sure of it. Size, view, everything. I knew exactly what I was going to do. Never mind lunch. I was going to preview that house. Right now.

The Pierpont house was on the west side of

town, on top of a hill. The view of the town and surrounding almond-tree-draped hillsides was spectacular. Mrs. Pierpont, a sweet-faced lady somewhere in middle age, was at home and grateful someone had finally taken the time to come look at her lovely home.

"We had it remodeled last year. We never dreamed George would be transferred, we've been here so long, but with this kind of promotion you don't say no, so I guess we're on our way."

She hesitated, obviously embarrassed. "Do you mind if I ask you a question?"

I knew what was coming. I didn't blame her, but I didn't want to answer. No choice presented itself, however. "Of course not."

"This is hard to say." She turned her ring round and round, not looking at me at all. "I know how difficult this last week has been for all of you, so much tragedy, but we can't help wondering— We really need to sell— Your office seems so— Well, we're wondering what is going to happen." She finally blurted it out and looked directly at me. "We like Sharon so much, and she has such a good reputation and all. She was so nice last Sunday, coming in all wet and not minding. I was afraid she'd ruin those beautiful blue shoes. Anyway, she explained everything so well and we don't want to lose her, but we did wonder if your office is going to keep going." She started on the ring again. "I don't mean to be rude, but…"

I wasn't feeling any more comfortable than she was. I'd had some of the same thoughts, but it didn't seem the time to tell her that, so I opted for vague and comforting.

"At this moment we don't know either, Mrs. Pierpont, but we are doing everything we can to keep the office open and to continue to provide our clients with the best possible service. The next few days should give us a better idea of what we need to do."

She looked doubtful, but nodded. "All right, then, we'll hear from Sharon in a few days?"

Praying I was telling the truth, I assured her she would. No wonder she was uncertain. First a client, next our secretary, both murdered, and one of our agents practically under arrest. I was surprised she was willing to wait a few days. I hoped Alice didn't have the same doubts. Perhaps I should be thinking of other possibilities, other offices, but I knew I couldn't be so disloyal. Sharon had been patient with me since I'd started, I could certainly return the favor. Besides, I wanted to know how all this turned out.

TWENTY-FIVE

SUSANNAH WAS ALREADY home. Her VW Rabbit was parked beside the back door, barely leaving me enough room to squeeze by. I stared at her open trunk. Dirty laundry spilled everywhere. I wondered if it was worth trying to make it into the garage, decided it wasn't, parked behind her and headed through the back door, loaded down with grocery bags.

"Hey." I hollered to be heard above the stereo while I looked for a clear space to set the sacks. My clean kitchen was now anything but! Evidently Susannah had made lunch.

"Hi, Mom."

She came through the door, carrying the remains of a glass of milk, gave me a peck on the cheek and started to unload the sacks. I watched her, amazed as always that I had produced this beautiful thing. We're both about five-six, but that's where the similarity ends. Her hair is dark, and curls luxuriously over her shoulders. Mine is somewhere between blond and brown with only a hint of a wave. Her eyes are violet, mine smoky blue, her lips and cheeks have a natural rosy hue, lovely against the slight tan she manages to maintain even in winter. Me? Well, thank goodness for Estée Lauder.

I ran upstairs to trade my wool slacks for jeans, stopped for a quick look in the full-length mirror, then turned around for a better view. Possibly, just possibly, middle age hadn't caught me yet. With this not-too-humble thought cheering me, I pulled my sweatshirt over my head, and rejoined Susannah in the kitchen.

Jake was investigating the empty sacks and Susannah was sitting at the kitchen table, drinking blackberry tea. She'd also discovered the Oreos.

"I've done two loads already," she announced. "Want some tea?"

"Sure." I sank gratefully into a chair. This morning, the last few days, had taken their toll. "I'm glad you're home. How many loads do you have left?"

"Quite a few." She didn't look at me, just jumped up to get my tea.

Suddenly suspicious, I said, "Susannah, how many people are you washing for?"

"Oh, Mom," was her reply, "you know how it is when you share an apartment. You take turns doing stuff."

Translated, that meant Susannah was the closest one to a washing machine that wasn't coin operated. Arguing about laundry was the last thing I needed, so I sat at the kitchen table and gratefully accepted the mug she handed me. She scooped Jake out of the paper sack he'd been killing, set him on her lap and offered him a piece of Oreo, which, to my surprise, he accepted. "Okay, tell me the latest."

I brought her up to date between sips of tea and a cookie or two. She was horrified, and satisfactorily concerned about my involvement.

"Who do you think did it?"

"I don't think it was Tom, even though Dan seems to have the most evidence against him."

"Dan?" Susannah raised both eyebrows. I ignored her.

"I think Benjamin's the most likely, although Ray Yarbourough isn't out of the race."

"Go slow. Remember, I don't know these people. Now, Tom's the young guy who worked in your office, the one with the pretty wife."

I nodded.

"Why don't you think he did it? You told me about his temper."

"I've never seen any signs of temper. Besides, Tom would never shoot Dottie, or anyone, in the back. That, I'm sure of."

"But Benjamin Lockwood would? Wait. Don't answer. I'll be right back."

She got up, pulled clothes out of the dryer,

dumped them in the basket, filled both the dryer and washer again, started them and slid back into her seat. "Okay. Go on."

College had taught her a lot. She'd done that in record time. "Where were we? Right. Benjamin. Would he shoot someone in the back." I thought about it. "He might. He's a fanatic on the Stop N Shop subject."

"But why Dottie? She sounds pretty harmless."

I told her my theory. She was impressed. "Yeah, something like that could have happened. But how do you find out?"

That stumped me. I had no idea. It didn't matter. Susannah was off in another direction.

"How about this Ray? He sounds pretty smarmy, and, if all that stuff about his license is true, he had plenty of motive."

"But shooting Dottie in the back. I don't know about that."

"He sounds like the type who wouldn't have the guts to shoot her if she was looking at him," Susannah observed callously. Unfortunately, she had a point.

"I wish it didn't have to be anybody, at least anybody I know."

"That doesn't appear to be a choice." The teakettle whistled. Susannah got up, poured water over fresh tea bags for us both, returned Jake to his sack and sat back down. "Aren't there any other possibilities? Some irate husband vowing vengeance?"

"Even if there were, he'd hardly be declaring vengeance on Dottie."

"Why does it have to be the same person?" Susannah asked. "Maybe someone else killed Dottie. After all, Hank was beaten to death. Dottie was shot. On all the TV programs, the killer uses the same method. It's called M.O."

"Why are you watching TV?" I asked in a mother-like voice. "Why aren't you studying?"

"I do that, too." She smiled at me complacently. "What do you think?"

"It's the same person." I was positive and I let it show in my voice. "There's some link between Hank and Dottie we're not seeing. Aunt Mary thinks so, too, and when we find that, we'll know who killed them."

"Wow," said Susannah. "So, what are you going to do?"

"Tonight I'm going to a Little Theater meeting. Hank and Dottie belonged, and everybody there knew them. Want to come?"

Susannah eyed me thoughtfully. "You mean you're going sleuthing, like one of the heroines in those books you read. Maybe I'd better go. Someone needs to keep tabs on you. Okay, it might even be fun."

She set her mug down and pushed back her chair in answer to the insistent buzzing of the dryer on the back porch. "I'll be V. I. Warshawski, you can be Mrs. Pollifax." Laughing uproariously at her not funny joke, she went back to her laundry. Mrs. Pollifax, indeed! Why, I'd never grown a geranium in my life.

I sat a little longer, savoring my tea, thinking up excuses why I shouldn't get up and start dinner, when I remembered Mr. Marburger. I'd better try Sharon again.

This time she answered on the second ring. I went into a long dissertation about my improvised trip around town with her client and finished with, "Where were you, anyway? You don't usually forget appointments."

"We didn't have one." Her voice was distant and stiff. "Only an understanding I'd try to fit him in if he found time, and I'm sure you did fine. Mr. Marburger is a most understanding man."

After deftly inserting that little barb, she went on, somewhat thoughtfully. "You're right about the Pierpont house, that might work. Mrs. Pierpont was there? What did she say?"

"She's understandably worried about us getting her house sold, but I held her hand a little. You'd better call her, Sharon. She really trusts you. She told me all about how you got caught in that downpour Sunday afternoon and got soaked but didn't mind, and how clearly you explained everything. I hope I get that good someday."

"Yes, well…" Sharon brushed off my compliment and abruptly changed the subject. "What have you heard about Tom? Has Dan arrested him?"

I told her I didn't think so, but was afraid it might happen soon, and went into my theory about Benjamin. She emphatically informed me Benjamin had never spoken to one of "her people" about Stop N Shop, and then, rather graphically described what she'd do to him if he tried. I doubted I was supposed to take her description literally, but, given her mood, decided I wouldn't bring up Ray. Sharon said she'd be in the office sometime on Saturday, and asked if I was coming in. I was noncommittal, and we hung up. It wasn't until I was staring at a couple of chicken breasts, wondering how creative I wanted to get, that I realized she hadn't offered any information about her mysterious absence. One more example of the tension these murders were creating in all of us. Dan had better find out who was responsible soon, or this town was going to come apart. *Of course, everyone can use a little help,* I thought cheerfully as I decided on chicken Parmesan, and reached for the olive oil. *Even Dan.*

TWENTY-SIX

"Brr," Susannah complained. "It's a lot colder here than in Santa Barbara. Is it always like this?"

"Yes, and it's hotter in the summer. Nice, isn't it?"

We were climbing the steps to the Veteran's Hall, on our way to The Little Theater meeting. Susannah wore a heavy jacket she'd found in my closet as well as a UCSB sweatshirt over her jeans. She'd pulled a knit hat down over her curls and had on heavy socks and L.L.Bean hiking boots. She looked like she was on her way to climb Everest.

"Spring is right around the corner," I told her cheerfully.

"Really. What corner is that?"

The room was stifling. We were both struggling out of our coats when Pat came up, a very tall, very blond, very good-looking young man right behind her. She gave me a quick hug, then looked inquiringly at Susannah.

"This is my daughter," I started as Pat said, "This is my son, Neil."

Neil was instantly at Susannah's side, helping

her off with her coat, his blond head bending down toward her dark one. She looked up at him with obvious interest as she stuffed her hat in her coat pocket.

"You can leave all that over there." Neil pointed toward some chairs lined up against the wall. He took her arm, as well as her coat, and they walked off.

Deserted, Pat and I watched their retreating backs.

"That didn't take long," Pat said wryly. "Drop your stuff on that pile and I'll introduce you around. We'll be starting in a few minutes."

People stood in little groups, talking, sipping coffee from white Styrofoam cups, and nibbling at the edges of the ubiquitous cookies that always show up at meetings. Tina waved at me. Tonight her fingernails were apple-green. They nicely matched her extra-tight miniskirt. She'd topped that with a voluminous blouse that contained twice as much material as her skirt and had finished the look with some sort of metal belt that clanked when she moved. I thought about Tina's mother, probably huddled in her kitchen, muttering into her coffee cup, praying her daughter would out-grow all this. Soon.

Pat headed toward Ruthie, who was talking with a man and woman I didn't recognize. I followed.

Ruthie gave me a large grin and a squeeze on the arm as we walked up. The man favored me with a friendly smile, the heavyset woman scowled.

Pat sighed, almost imperceptibly, and started the introductions. "Ellen, this is Dr. Carl Bennington. He's the president of The Little Theater group, and in his spare time is a small-animal veterinarian and my husband."

The shorter, slightly balding version of Neil pumped my hand. "How nice to meet you. You haven't had the greatest homecoming this past week, but I hope you have some fun with us."

I pumped his hand right back, and decided instantly Jake had a new doctor.

Pat went on with the introductions. "This is Amelia Williams. She's the secretary for our group."

There was an undercurrent in Pat's voice that made me take a better look at Amelia, who still scowled from under carefully plucked eyebrows. The effects of gravity showed in her face, or maybe it was discontent that pulled down the corners of her mouth, but one too many hot fudge sundaes had created the wattles that swayed over the neck of her cashmere sweater.

"So you're the one that found the bodies." She hurled each word at me. "Ruthie says you were there when they took Tom Chandler off, too.

You've been busy since you came back to town. Any other juicy little pies you're planning to get your fingers in?"

I found myself speechless. Who was this woman? What did she have against me?

"Just like your mother and your aunts, aren't you? Can't leave well enough alone." Turning her back on me, she said to the group in general, "It looks like Dan Dunham finally got something right. I've always known Tom Chandler was no good. He's got an uncontrollable temper, and now it's caught up with him." She gave a self-satisfied nod that set the wattles going and glanced over her shoulder at me with another glare.

I was nonplussed, embarrassed and furious. What had I done to be on the receiving end of all that spite? There was a tug on my sleeve. Pat, deeply flushed, pulled me away.

Amelia had quite an audience gathered round, listening intently. Carl vainly tried to change the subject. "Time to get started, everyone," he kept saying, but Amelia wasn't about to relinquish her place at center stage. On she went, relating more of Tom's sins, past and present.

Curious looks brushed across my back as Pat dragged me into the far corner with the coats. Tina and Ruthie were right behind, and they all immediately started to console me.

"That vicious old bat." Ruthie patted my arm with a little more force than necessary. "It's a wonder she doesn't choke on her own venom."

"I'm sorry, Ellen." Pat, usually smiling Pat, scowled. "I should have warned you about Amelia. She's our cross to bear." She looked back toward the center of the room and sighed. "Poor Carl. She must have cornered him right away, and he was having such a good day."

"Carl hates her." Ruthie acted as if she was confiding a deeply guarded secret. I looked back over at the group. From the rigid stance of Carl's back, that was no secret.

"But why me?" I asked, still shaken. "I've never seen the woman before."

"It's your Aunt Mary," Ruthie said.

"My—what?"

"Amelia likes to direct," Pat said, distaste obvious. "People, organizations, fundraisers, she doesn't care as long as she's in charge. Only, she's not too fond of work."

"She's great at causing fights," Ruthie observed.

That, I could believe. "What does that have to do with me?"

"Your Aunt Mary McGill works her tail off, gets everything and everybody organized and won't tolerate fights. So, when a chairman of anything gets chosen, Amelia's out, Mary's in." Ruthie smiled broadly. "Our dear Amelia hates Mary, you're her niece, so you get hated, too."

"Mary doesn't belong to our group—" Pat sighed, as if that was a regrettable fact "—so, of course, Amelia joined. She keeps trying to run everything, but, so far, we've beaten her down."

"I'll bet she keeps trying." I took another look at the venomous Amelia. "What was all that about Tom? She makes it sound like he blows up all the time. Is that true?"

Pat and Ruthie glanced at each other. Ruthie replied, looking troubled, "Sort of. It's not that he gets mad a whole lot, but when he does, he really blows." Then she quickly added, "He cools down real fast."

"Tom beat up Kevin the other night." Tina. I'd forgotten she was there, and whirled around to look at her. Ruthie and Pat stared at her also.

"When?" Ruthie demanded.

"How do you know?" asked Pat.

"Who's Kevin?" I added.

"Kevin is Amelia's son," Pat answered.

"Kevin's a…"

"Ruthie," Pat warned.

"Well, anyone who punches out Kevin is okay in my book," Ruthie declared.

"Will someone please tell me what's wrong with Kevin and why Tom hit him?" I said impatiently.

"Kevin likes to harass women." Pat looked like she'd taken a mouthful of sour milk. "He corners you, starts off telling dirty jokes, goes on to innuendoes, makes sure you're embarrassed, then gets explicit. It's hard to get away from him without making a scene, and, of course, that's what he counts on."

"Yeah," Tina said. "My sister saw it."

Tina lost me, but not Pat. "Your sister saw Tom hit Kevin?"

"At the Blue Beetle, down by the college. Kevin was telling Nicole a joke, and Tom landed him right on the floor. Jumped right on top of him. He really punched Kevin out." She giggled. "Wish I'd seen it. I can't stand Kevin." That seemed to make it unanimous.

Carl had finally gotten most of the group away from Amelia and was calling for the meeting to start, but I wasn't quite ready to let go of this discussion.

"Are you saying Tom's temper is so bad he hits people on a regular basis?"

"No, of course not," Pat said rather defensively. "It's nothing more than being a little hotheaded sometimes. Dan's wrong. Tom wouldn't kill anybody."

"If it wasn't for that gun," Ruthie said wistfully. "It'd be nice to think someone stole it from him, but how could anyone know he had one, or that he kept it in his car?"

"I think we better sit down." Pat sounded a little nervous. "Carl's frowning, not a good sign."

Tina started toward the chairs, then turned back and offhandedly said, "Benjamin Lockwood knew about Tom's gun and where he kept it."

"Wait." Ruthie grabbed Tina by the hand and pulled her through the double doors into the empty hallway. Pat and I hurried after them.

"Okay, give." Ruthie had Tina up against the wall like someone from a scene in an old gangster movie, flanked by an astounded Pat and a fascinated me. "How do you know about Tom's gun?"

Maybe it was the bad light, the shock of our sudden interrogation or just a reflection from Tina's skirt, but her complexion took on a slightly greenish tinge. "They were talking about it," she stammered.

"Who was talking about what when?" Ruthie pressed.

"Just a minute." Pat pulled Ruthie back a little. "Tina, tell us how you know about the gun." Her voice was calm, quiet, obviously trying to steady the thoroughly rattled girl.

"I was at the Emporium, looking for boots." Tina stopped and eyed Ruthie as if she thought she'd be attacked at any moment.

"Go on," Pat encouraged.

"Tom was there, talking to Benjamin about guns, hunting rifles or something. Tom said he had a handgun and had Benjamin ever tried one."

"What'd Benjamin say?" Ruthie was trying to close in again.

"I don't know. I wasn't listening. What do I care about stupid old guns?" Tina was edging toward the door but Ruthie was too fast for her.

"What else?"

"Nothing else." A slight flush crept up Tina's cheeks, replacing the light green color. "Except Dottie told Tom it wasn't safe to carry guns around, unlocked, in cars and stuff. She was pretty insistent. Tom laughed."

"Dottie? Dottie was there?" It was Ruthie who asked, but we all stared at her, trying to absorb this.

"What's so unusual about that? There's no place else to shop in this town." Tina ducked under Ruthie's arm, flounced through the double doors into the auditorium, blond hair and green skirt both bouncing in indignation.

"What do you think?" Pat looked as confused as I felt.

"Plain as black and white." Ruthie certainly wasn't confused. "I don't know why I didn't see it before. Benjamin killed Hank in a rage, then he stole Tom's gun and shot Dottie because he knew she knew he knew Tom had one. The old reprobate."

"That doesn't make sense," Pat exclaimed. I didn't say anything. I was still trying to unscramble Ruthie's sentence.

"Ruthie, think. Dottie was shot for some other reason entirely, not because she knew about the gun. Ellen already told us Ray knew about it, and if Tom talked so freely, probably half the town knew. No, this only means Benjamin could have taken it, nothing more.

"Do you agree, Ellen?"

I nodded. Pat was right. We hadn't proved anything, but we had removed one "suppose." Benjamin knew about the gun and where to find it. If only I could remove a few more "supposes."

We trailed silently back through the double doors into the auditorium. Pat looked worried, Ruthie confused. Now that her theory had been blown apart. I mulled over all this new information, wondering if it meant anything, and if so, what? I tried to sit myself on a flimsy folding chair without making a racket and almost missed Carl's announcement.

"There will be a memorial service for Dottie Fielding tomorrow morning at St. Stephen's Episcopal Church, at ten o'clock. She will be buried in the mid-west, with her family, so we thought this would be best. I hope all of you can come and, please, tell anyone else who might not have heard. This has been a hard week for all of us, a shocking week. This is the least we can do to honor a good friend. Now, about this year's musical."

The arguments flew fast and furious. It seemed the selection committee wanted to do *Man of La Mancha*. Several others, led by Amelia, surprise, surprise, wanted to do *Cats*. Tempers ran high for a while, and I got caught up in the drama of the floor fight. *Man of La Mancha* won.

"I'm exhausted," I told Pat as the meeting broke up. "The U.S. Senate is tame compared to this. Is it always like that?"

"No, thank God. Only when it's time to choose a new play or musical. I told you Amelia likes to run things. This evening you had the special treat of seeing her in action."

"But she lost."

"Yes," Pat replied, and we both laughed.

I looked around for Susannah. She was across the room with Neil, who was helping her on with her coat.

"Mom. You don't mind going home alone, do you? Neil and I thought we'd go have coffee."

"Denny's. It's the only place open." Neil peered

earnestly at me. "I won't keep her out late, so you don't have to stay up."

Now, that was funny. Susannah lived in an apartment with three other girls who didn't, I was sure, keep track of her hours. I doubted if the domineering-mother act would work on her any longer. Not that it ever had. However, for appearances' sake, I said, "No, I don't mind. Be careful driving."

Promising he would indeed be careful, Neil hustled her out, leaving me looking back at Pat's smiling face. She walked over to me.

"That was quick. Do you think they were struck by lightning when we weren't looking? Anyway, how about stopping by our place for coffee? I'll even add a little something extra to it."

"Thanks," I said, "but not tonight. I'd love a rain check though."

"You've got it. See you tomorrow morning?"

Dottie's memorial. Of course. Assuring Pat I'd be there, I headed home.

My exhaustion turned to restlessness the minute I walked through my door. Why hadn't I taken Pat up on her invitation, I thought, as I listened to the quiet of my house. I needed someone to talk to. The clock told me it was too late to call Aunt Mary. I didn't know Dan's home number, and that didn't feel right anyway. I turned on my TV, but couldn't get into David Letterman. Finally I made myself a cup of Susannah's blackberry tea, took it, Jake and my newest library book up to bed. The red light on my answering machine was blinking. *I'm not pushing that button,* I thought, *not after the last time.* Curiosity was too strong, and finally I reached out and pressed it. It was the TV station, saying they'd been trying to find me for two days. They wanted an interview. I thought about it for a minute, then moved Jake off my pillow, climbed in and opened my book. So much for fame.

TWENTY-SEVEN

WHEN I WOKE it was a bright, sunny Saturday morning. A quick check of Susannah's room showed her still asleep, an extra quilt pulled up around her head. I turned up the heat, put Jake out and started the coffee.

A glance at the clock told me it wasn't too early to call Aunt Mary. I caught her going out the door.

"I'm going to the church to help get everything ready for Dottie's memorial service. I've ordered flowers in both our names. You owe me twenty-five dollars. We're only going to have coffee, brownies, that kind of thing. I think that will be all right."

Since neither Dottie's family nor Dottie would be attending, I thought it was more than all right. I wasn't sure we needed to send flowers. Who were we sending them to? But some things never change, so flowers and brownies we would have.

I contented myself with saying, "I've got several things to tell you, but they can wait. I'll see you right after the service." I wanted to ask what she was wearing, but decided to wait and see. Surprise is so much more fun.

Susannah came yawning down the stairs. I started to say good morning when the phone rang. It was Dan.

"Ellie, sorry I didn't get to call you yesterday, but life's been a little hectic. How'd you like The Little Theater meeting?"

"How did you know?"

"Listen," he said, ignoring my question, "I only have a minute. Are you doing anything tonight? I have two tickets for the jazz concert at the Performing Arts Center. Want to go?"

"Sure." I was caught completely off guard. Why did I feel like a high school girl being asked on her first date? Or nowadays is it junior high? "That sounds wonderful. Ah, what time..."

"Early. I thought we'd have dinner over on the coast first. About six? One condition though."

Here it came. "What condition?"

"No murders, okay? No talk of murder, no thinking of murder. I'm up to my—elbows in these murders and I need a night off."

I laughed, agreed and hung up.

Susannah stood in the middle of the kitchen, wrapped in the quilt, which spilled from her shoulders to pool on the floor. She kicked it aside and plopped down in one of the chairs.

"What was that all about?"

Suddenly I was stricken with guilt, and turned

away to hide my face. Susannah, my only child, had come home to spend the weekend with her mother, and I had accepted a date! With a man not her father!

"That was Dan Dunham. Remember? I told you about him." I tried to hide behind the orange juice pitcher. "He wants me to go to a jazz concert with him tonight. Do you want eggs or cereal?"

"The guy who used to live next door when you were growing up?"

I nodded miserably, trying to think what kind of excuse I could give Dan for not going with him.

"He asked you out?"

"Yes, but…"

"Way to go, Mom." Susannah reached for the cereal box.

"You don't mind?" I was frozen with surprise, pitcher halfway to the table. Susannah reached up, took it from me and poured a glass.

"Of course not. It's way past time you started seeing someone. You're not married anymore, you know. And you still look pretty good." She took a large swallow and shuddered. "Ugh, sour." She set the glass on the table and went on. "You were great the whole time Dad was playing around, and you were terrific during the divorce. Now it's your turn."

I sank into a chair opposite her, amazed. How

long had she known about her father's extracurricular activities? Should I have protected her more? Was she scarred for life? All this was swirling through my head when Susannah calmly announced, "Besides, Neil asked me out, so now I won't have to worry about you being alone. Do we have any English muffins?"

So much for being scarred. I stuck muffins in the toaster.

"I'm going to Dottie's memorial service." I had one eye on the clock, the other on this surprising daughter who was slicing a banana on her cereal. "Do you want to come?"

"No, thanks. I've got a bunch of homework, and I need to finish up that laundry so I'll be free tonight. Do you want anything washed?" Susannah smiled at me much too knowingly.

I muttered, "I don't think so," and, munching my own muffin, went upstairs to shower and change, a mass of conflicting emotions.

The memorial service was short, but moving. Several people told incidents from Dottie's life, including the rector, who had known her well. The choir did a beautiful job, and one of the members of The Little Theater sang "Amazing Grace," Dottie's favorite hymn.

I tried to catch Aunt Mary in the church hall as

she buzzed by. I got Pat instead, who handed me a cup of coffee.

"I understand our kids are going out tonight. I haven't seen Neil this smitten since he had a crush on his third-grade teacher."

"My mother used to say one of the nicest things about small-town living was you always knew who your daughter was dating." I smiled at the thought. "She was talking about families, of course. I never thought it was so wonderful, but now I see what she meant."

"I think it's one of those things that can be a curse or a joy. It depends on which side of the generation gap you're on."

Aunt Mary appeared, carrying a tray of brownies, which she set on the already overloaded dessert table.

"What are you two giggling about? Excellent service. Dottie would have been pleased."

"Come over here. We've got things to tell you."

I pulled her away toward a quiet corner followed by an awestruck Pat. I couldn't blame her. Today, Aunt Mary had outdone herself. She had on a vivid magenta silk dress topped with a huge lace collar she'd fastened with a beautiful old cameo pin I thought I recognized as my grandmother's. Her stockings were white, her shoes lime-green, with straps. She was wearing the same hat that had gone to Hank's funeral, only now it was topped with bright red plastic cherries. The effect took some getting used to.

She listened carefully until I finished. "I don't think that's much. So Benjamin knew Tom had a gun. The young idiot. Why people think they need to keep guns in unlocked places… Anyway, just because Benjamin knew where it was doesn't mean he took it. Besides, if Tom talked that freely, plenty of others must have known about it. Ray certainly did, not that I think he'd have the gumption. No, we still don't have any reason, any factual reason for Benjamin to want to kill Dottie." She paused, looked thoughtful for a moment before she went on. "I have to admit, though, he's sure been busy giving himself a motive for Hank's death. I still think there's some kind of link between Hank and Dottie we're not seeing, and when Dan—" she paused again, and gave me another meaningful look "—finds it, he'll find the real murderer."

Aunt Mary hustled off toward the kitchen, picking up an empty coffeepot on her way.

"She's really something." Pat took my empty cup and stacked it with her own on the dirty-dish tray. "Not too subtle though. I think she wants you to quit snooping."

"I haven't been snooping. I've only come up

with a couple of theories. Besides, I found both bodies. It's a little hard not to feel involved. She's the one who keeps saying it couldn't be Tom Chandler."

"I wonder if Dan knows about Tom's fight with Kevin."

"If he doesn't, he'll find out."

"It's too bad Tom couldn't have chosen another time to flatten the little creep," Pat observed, looking at her watch. "I've got to go. One of Carl's assistants is home with flu, he had an emergency surgery and I'm supposed to be answering phones. Call me."

People were drifting away, and it seemed a good time for me to leave as well. I caught sight of Ray getting into his Lincoln. He had sat through the service wooden faced, while Sharon, several rows behind him, had once or twice looked like she was going to lose control. There was no sign of Tom or Nicole. I didn't like to think what that meant.

I needed to pick up some information for my appointment with Alice Ives tomorrow, so I headed for the office. I found myself wanting all my errands done, so I would be home in plenty of time to go through my closet. I had no idea what I was going to wear tonight, and was sorely irritated by the fact that I cared.

Dan, I thought crossly. Aunt Mary certainly

had a lot of confidence in him, but right now I couldn't see why. He seemed to have made up his mind Tom was guilty of both murders, and neither Aunt Mary nor I agreed with him. Tonight I'd ask him— Damn. We'd agreed. No talk of murder. Tonight. Clothes. Hum. Perhaps something new? I'd just stop in at the Emporium, and if I ran into Benjamin, well, what would be more natural than a little conversation?

I was in luck. There was Benjamin, waiting on a harried-looking young woman with three small children in tow. Evidently she'd been buying shoes, as the oldest, a boy about five, was admiring his feet encased in new, high-topped black tennis shoes. She was trying to shove a bulky parcel in the backpack attached to a stroller, placate the screaming baby it contained and keep her toddler from pulling over the rack of ties she was fingering thoughtfully. She finally got herself and her charges to the door, which I held open for her. She flashed me a tired and somewhat embarrassed smile, murmured, "Thanks," and escaped.

"My." I returned to the shoe department and a dejected-looking Benjamin. "That really takes me back. Every pair of shoes I had when I was little came from here. I can't remember ever going anywhere else."

A slight exaggeration, actually a pretty large

one, but I needed something to get a conversation going. It worked, too. Benjamin replied sadly, "Young people today don't think like that, what with new stores and all the rest of the tomfoolery goin' on in this town."

"Don't be silly. You'll still have tons of customers, even if Stop N Shop does come." I cast a surreptitious glance at the miserable selection and the empty aisleways, and knew I'd lied.

"I don't know, Ellen. This town's changin', and it's not for the best. Makes me so angry I could burst. You lookin' for somethin' in particular?"

"Well, a sweater maybe, sort of dressy…" I stopped, appalled, as Benjamin pulled a blue denim-colored thing, dripping with silver fringe, off the rack.

"This'd look real good on you, Ellen. They tell me women really like this stuff right now. Got boots?"

"Maybe something a little less—ah—conspicuous." Staring at that sweater made me feel I should burst into a chorus of "Stand By Your Man" any minute. I mentally flipped through my closet once more.

Benjamin snorted and shoved the sweater back on the rack. "See, even you, Ellen. No pleasin' anyone anymore. I suppose when that new store comes you'll desert me too. Everyone wants new, somethin' different. Look at Sharon Harper. Comes back to town, takes over her father's perfectly good office, an office folks could trust, and starts changin' things. 'Development,' she calls it." He was flipping sweaters back and forth on the rack, faster and faster as he got more agitated. "First that big market, now this Stop N Shop, and I hear tell now she wants some big chain restaurant here. What's wrong with the bowling alley coffee shop, that's what I want to know. All this changin' things gets folks riled up, confused, then terrible things happen."

"What kind of terrible things?" I held my breath; sure Benjamin was worked up enough to let something slip. "You mean like what happened to Hank and Dottie?"

"Hank was a good friend of mine, and I'll miss him, but he never should've tried to vote for that darn store. Real sad."

Now we were getting somewhere, I thought. "How about Dottie?"

"Dottie Fielding?" Benjamin peered at me, a cagey look creeping over his face. "Dottie was a nosy woman, never could leave well enough alone in all the years I knew her. Guess she got herself in the middle of something she couldn't get out of. You goin' to buy somethin' or not, Ellen? I ain't got all day to stand here and gossip with women, you know."

I remembered just in time he was an old man, and a not-too-rational one. "I'll look a little more," I said, and moved the sweaters around. Benjamin scurried off. As soon as he was out of sight, I escaped to the sanctuary of my car. I sat for a few minutes, trying to swallow my indignation as well as digest our conversation. The old reprobate! I was more and more sure he was the leading candidate for Hank, but still had to find out why Dottie? *Nosy woman.* That sounded like my theory could be correct. If Dottie had been trying to keep Benjamin from talking to the land partners, if she had been trying to stop him from telling lies, "nosy" would be the kindest thing he'd say. But would he, did he, do anything? I sighed as I started my engine. I wished I knew what Dan was doing, what he was thinking. I wouldn't find out tonight. But there was always tomorrow. With that cheery thought, I headed for the office.

Sharon was the only one in. She was looking through the files in the cabinet behind Dottie's desk.

"Hi. Did you ever get in touch with Mr. Marburger?"

Evidently she hadn't heard me come in for she started, then whirled around, papers from the file she was holding flying everywhere. She looked at me, ashen faced, and took a deep breath. "Oh, Ellen. It's you."

Who did she think it was? "I'm sorry, I didn't mean to startle you. Here, let me help you."

I started to pick up papers, but Sharon was already on her knees, waving me away. "Never mind, I can get them." She scooped them all into a folder, got up and dropped everything into her briefcase, which was open on Dottie's desk. "I didn't expect you today, Ellen. I didn't expect anyone today." She leaned against the desk, as if she needed it to support her. "I think Tom's back at the police station, answering more questions, and Nicole's useless. I haven't seen Ray. Have you?"

"This morning, at the service."

"The blasted phone keeps ringing," Sharon went on. "All clients wanting to know if the office is going to stay open. Of course it's going to stay open, but they've got to give us a few days. As soon as I get us reorganized— You wouldn't like to stay and answer phones, would you?" She didn't say this with much hope, and only shrugged when I said no.

"I came down to collect some information for Alice Ives. I'm still going over there tomorrow to list her house." I crossed my fingers, hoping that would stay true.

"Oh." Sharon's face brightened. "Want some help?"

Did I! The phones went on answering service, the computers clicked on, printers spit out comparable sales and listings, and soon I had enough information to convince even twittery Alice of what we needed to do.

"Thanks, Sharon." I clutched the reams of information I had. "I really appreciate this."

"No problem." Sharon snapped her briefcase shut and headed for the door. "Sort through all that, put the marketing information in one file, and all the forms and disclosures you need in another. You'll be fine."

It didn't take long to finish. I stood up, stretched, collected my folders and started to leave. My hand reached for the door handle, but it opened before I could touch it, and there stood Ray.

"Oh." I gasped and took a step back.

"What's the matter with you?" Ray's face looked tense and drawn, but angry, too.

"Nothing. I was just, ah, what are you doing here?"

"I work here." He sounded bitter. Rude and bitter. "A word most people don't seem to understand."

"For heaven's sake, Ray." I was stung by the accusation in his voice. "This has hardly been a normal week. Hank, then Dottie, now Tom's a suspect, it hasn't been easy."

"Maybe not." He sounded as if saying that was a huge concession. "What are you doing here?"

I took another step back. He took one toward me. "Getting information for Alice Ives." I wondered if I could edge around him and get out the door.

"Right. You're supposed to list her house, aren't you? Need some help?" He reached out for the files I was clutching to my chest. "Let's see what you've done."

"No." I knew I was stammering but couldn't help it. "Sharon helped me, it's fine, and I've got to…" I darted behind Dottie's desk, thinking only I had to get away from him, and slipped. Ray grabbed my arm, a little too hard, and snatched my files from me.

"You're going to drop all this stuff if you don't put it in your briefcase." He didn't look as if he wanted to be helpful. He still looked angry and sour. I nodded, not trusting myself to speak, and headed back toward my own desk and the briefcase I'd forgotten. He followed me and handed me the folders. I thrust them in and started to snap the briefcase shut, when I realized Ray was still right behind me. I stiffened, and let my hand tighten on the handle of the case. If I swung it…

"This yours?" Ray handed me a piece of paper. "It probably fell out of your folder."

It was a piece of Harper's Land Sale stationery, with a list of names on it. Also one footprint. Mine. I stared at it, confused. It was the same list of names Dottie had left for Hank. Nice, neat list of partners down the left side, complete with addresses and phone numbers. Opposite some of the names, new ones, handwritten, no addresses, no phone numbers. This was what I'd slipped on, but what was it doing on our office floor?

"That yours, or not?" Ray demanded, holding out his hand for the paper.

"Right. Sure." I stuffed the paper in Alice's file and snapped the case shut. "Thanks." My hand was shaking. What was Ray going to do now? He turned, went to his own desk and picked up the phone. My knees went weak with relief. I grabbed my case and ran out the door.

I STOOD IN FRONT OF a closet again, only this time it was mine. I pulled clothes out of it, examined them and shoved them right back in. Susannah and Jake sat on my bed, propped up against my pillows, watching.

"I don't know what the weather's going to be like at the beach."

"Warmer than here," she replied, pulling my quilt over her legs.

"How dressed up do people get for these things?" I threw a skirt on the bed, slammed the closet closed, and pulled open the sweater drawer.

"The Performing Arts Center is at the college." Susannah scratched Jake between the ears. He purred. "Jazz. Students. Wear anything." She watched me with a mixture of curiosity and amusement. "You really like this guy, don't you?"

"Of course. We grew up together. Here. What do you think of this?" I had put together a neat little outfit of gray wool skirt, demure white blouse, navy blazer and low-heeled pumps.

"You're not applying for a job."

I put everything back in the closet.

"Don't you have any nice pants?" She disentangled herself from Jake and the quilt. "I've got to get ready. You're going to introduce me to this Dan before I go back, aren't you? As the only child, it's my responsibility to pass judgment." Chuckling, she drifted out of my room and down the hall.

I thought about throwing my shoe at her, but instead pulled out my best slacks, topped them with my favorite oversized turtleneck sweater, the one that matches my eyes, found a scarf and settled for loafers and pant socks. A little extra attention to makeup and hair, and I was ready when the doorbell rang.

"Nice," was all he said when he saw me, but it was enough. "Do you like clam chowder? There's a place in Morro Bay that makes the best, and we have time. That okay?"

The drive over to the coast takes about thirty minutes and winds through a narrow canyon before it drops down beside the big Morro rock. We headed for a small place on the pier, and took seats at a window table overlooking the bay. The fishing boats were tied up securely for the night, their empty masts casting long shadows as they lazily bobbed up and down. The gulls had found their evening perches, and a faint breeze brought the tangy scent of salt water and seaweed.

We were early. Only a couple of other tables were occupied, and the low light of the candle on ours, reflecting against the white of the cloth, created an island that we alone inhabited as we smiled at each other.

"Hi," sounded a voice, neatly shattering the mood. "Menus? Been here before? Can I get you a drink?"

Throwing cholesterol caution to the wind, we ordered the chowder, deep-fried halibut with french fries, cole slaw and a half bottle of wine, with coffee to follow.

We talked. We talked about everything. I had forgotten how much fun that could be, to talk, to discuss, to argue a little. Brian and I had reached the point where our conversation was limited to "has the paper arrived?" or "will you be home to dinner? No?" I could have gone on talking for hours, but Dan looked at his watch, motioned for the check and we were on our way inland.

The music was wonderful. I don't know what I had been expecting, but not this exciting blend of professionals and students. As we were leaving, we met several couples Dan knew and chatted with them for a few minutes. I wondered if their curious glances were sizing us up as a possible couple, or if they recognized me as the notorious newcomer who tripped over dead bodies.

On the way home, I felt euphoric. The good food, excellent music, warm car and comfortable companionship were doing their job. I leaned my head back on the seat, turning slightly to smile at Dan. He smiled back. His sandy hair, lightly frosted with gray, fell over his left eye, just as it used to. I felt an almost overwhelming urge to reach up and gently smooth it back.

"Having fun, Ellie?" he asked unnecessarily. He offered his right arm and I moved over, without even thinking, to nestle against him. We were back in town, I realized sleepily, as I allowed myself to burrow even more deeply into Dan's side. It seemed so natural to be here beside him, almost home, almost asleep.

I woke up. I could feel myself stiffen, and I pulled away. Dan removed his arm and looked over at me. Was there a question in those slightly raised eyebrows? What question? What should I say?

All the years Brian and I had been married, I had never played around. Brian had, plenty. I'd been propositioned by his friends, advised by their wives to have my fun while there was still time, but I never did. It all seemed so tawdry. And now, I didn't know what to do. Would Dan expect to come in? More to the point, would he expect to stay? The idea had appeal, a lot more than I had expected. That kiss the other night had started me thinking about feelings, desires I'd resolutely buried for years. But I wasn't ready. It was too soon after my divorce. Or something.

We pulled up in front of my house. I felt frozen in my seat. Dan got out, moved around to my door and opened it.

"Are you going to get out?" He took me by the hand and gave me a little pull. He gently propelled me up the front stairs, opened his hand for my key, slid open the door, reached around and turned on the hallway light. His face shone dimly against the dark of the porch, his expression tender, I was sure, and that damn hair was over his eye again. Maybe…

"Did you have a good time, Ellie?"

"Oh, yes. I had a wonderful time. The food, the music, everything…"

"Good," he interrupted. "So did I. Want to do it again? Soon?"

Did I! "I'd love to."

"Good," he said again. He slid his arm around me, pulled me close, and gave me a very hard, very long kiss. For a second or two I didn't respond, but it didn't take long. Just as I was getting into it, he let me go.

"I'll call you. Don't forget to bolt the door." He turned me gently and pushed me inside, then pulled the door closed behind him. I heard the car door slam, the engine start, and the car drive away.

I was paralyzed. The only thing moving was my emotions, taking turns turning cartwheels over each other. Sweet, thoughtful Dan. How like him to understand, to give me time to—what? Did he know how vulnerable I still felt? Was that it? That kiss hadn't felt neighborly. It had felt— It had left me— I hadn't felt like this for a long time. I slipped off one shoe, then the other, and stared some more at the closed door. Had I wanted

Dan to—come in? No, of course not. Yes, very much yes.

"Damn," I said out loud. "How am I supposed to know what I want?" I bent down and picked up my shoes as Jake came out of the living room. He looked at the shoes, then me, and fled up the stairs.

"Isn't that nice. I can't even keep the cat in the same room with me."

I had meant to make tea, but suddenly it seemed so tame. The brandy bottle sat beside the wine rack, looking at me. I don't much like brandy, but tonight I was having some. I poured a tiny glass and then had no idea what to do. Susannah wasn't back yet, so I couldn't talk to her. The late night news would depress me more, and a cold shower didn't sound a bit good. Finally, I took my glass upstairs, shoved Jake over and propped myself up with my book. Susannah would be home soon, and we'd have a nice long girl chat. *At least,* I thought as I opened the book, *I kept my bargain. We never mentioned murder.*

TWENTY-EIGHT

SOMEWHERE A CHILD was crying. Years of conditioning worked, and I instantly sat straight up. Freed, Jake stalked to the other side of the bed where he curled into a ball, tucking his injured tail under him.

"Well, if you kept on your own side, I'd never have laid on it." I slid back down, pulling the covers up over my face. It was Sunday and I had no intention of getting up early. However, the seductive smell of fresh coffee was on the air and it seemed to be coming my way. It was right under my nose.

"Mom," whispered a voice, "are you awake?"

"I am now." I sighed and struggled to sit up, not an easy task as Susannah was now on the edge of the bed balancing two coffee cups.

"Here." She handed me mine as I pushed a pillow behind my back. "How was last night? Did you have fun?"

"Humn, yes. Lots of fun." I allowed the memory to warm me along with the coffee. "How about you?"

Susannah watched me, one eyebrow raised questioningly. "Did he kiss you?"

"Susannah! Really."

"I knew he would."

"Yeah?" I did not want to go further down that path. "Did Neil kiss you?"

"Of course." Her smile was the kind that makes a mother's heart turn cold. "We went to a party at one of Neil's friend's house. Lots of people said their folks knew you when you lived here before. I even met one girl who claims she's a third cousin or something. Is that possible?"

"Entirely possible. I should have brought you here more often when you were little. Is Neil, ah, nice?"

"Neil's great," wasn't exactly what I was looking for, but before I could ask a more pointed question Susannah was off on another track. "I don't think Dad liked small towns very much, but I do. This one, anyway." She switched again. "Did you know Neil's going to vet school at Davis next year? He's already been admitted and everything. He's going to be an equine vet." She smiled at me serenely. "That's one who takes care of horses."

"I know what *equine* means. That's not what I want to know about him."

"Quit worrying, Mom." This time the grin was wide. "He's a gentleman. Too bad, huh."

"No." I struggled to disentangle myself from the quilt. Susannah got up, freeing me, and headed out of the room.

"Where are you going?"

"To shower. Neil's picking me up. We're going to look at a horse."

"You don't know anything about horses. You don't even like them."

"I do now." Her grin was wicked. "I thought you might like to fix us both some breakfast. I've sure missed your pancakes."

I'd walked right into that one. I pulled my old robe around me and descended the stairs.

It didn't take Susannah long. She had barely entered the kitchen, poured into tight jeans topped with her baggiest sweatshirt, when there was a loud knock on the back door. A booted, cowboy-hatted Neil appeared.

"I just ate," he responded to my invitation of eggs, bacon, pancakes, juice and milk, "but, maybe a little."

He hung his hat on the chair he pulled out and stared admiringly at Susannah, who smiled demurely back at him over her coffee cup. There was more to that smile than excitement over visiting a horse. I jabbed at the bacon. *Let her grow up,* I silently lectured myself. As if I had a choice, I snarled back.

A little breakfast turned into a lot, but they finally finished and left, talking about all matters equine.

I sighed, looked at the remaining pancake batter and allowed myself to be tempted. I poured the last of the coffee and opened the Sunday paper.

The rest of the morning passed quickly and peacefully. I caught myself with barely enough time to make my appointment with Alice.

She was glad to see me and, as usual, chattered away in several different directions at once. Finally she said, "Don't you want to see the house, dear? It's been a long time since you were here last."

She was right. Her daughter, Corinne, and I had been friends of a sort through high school, but I had been an infrequent visitor even then. It was time for a review.

Touring that house was a true treat. It was older than mine or Aunt Mary's, and larger. The entry seemed designed to set off the beautiful stairway with its intricately carved newel posts. The formal living room opened off to the right, French doors separating it from the dining room. There was a library, without many books, and a solarium with wicker furniture and a jungle of plants. No modern updates in the kitchen, and the traditional damp, steep steps led into the basement. I didn't inves-

tigate. A small, somewhat dark bathroom downstairs, a large, light one, with an antique claw-foot
tub, served all three upstairs bedrooms. All in all,
a charming old home for someone with a taste for
history. I wondered how many buyers we would
be able to tempt.

The tour ended in the kitchen where I spread
out my materials on the round oak table. The most
important thing was to establish a sales price, and
to show Alice how much money she would realize from the sale. A lot of questions needed to be
asked, and I needed her attention. Not an easy
task. I was fairly sure the house had no mortgage,
but I needed to find out.

"Oh, no, dear. We haven't had a mortgage for
years. Simon didn't believe in them, you know. I
won't put one on my house in Florida either. But
I want something smaller there, a condo maybe.
I think I'll try golf, everyone says it's so healthy.
Have you ever played? Is it hard? It doesn't look
hard, just hitting that little ball into a cup, then
riding around in that darling cart, and the grass
is always so nice…"

After several such side trips, I arrived at a sales
price I thought sounded pretty reasonable. Alice
agreed. I pulled the listing form from the file, and
out came the paper I had slipped on in the office.

"What's this, dear?" Alice picked it up. "Why,

there's my name. And that nice Mr. Cameron, who bought my shares."

"When did you meet him?" I was concentrating on filling in the form correctly, and only gave Alice half my attention.

"Oh, I've never met him, but I'm sure he's nice. Sharon said he was. He gave me such a generous offer for my shares. You know, dear, Simon always said we'd never make a dime on that investment, but we did very well."

"Oh? How long ago did you sell them? Sign here, Alice." I handed her the pen and indicated the correct line.

"Not quite a year ago." Alice handed me back the pen. "Right after Simon's death, but before that new store, what's its name? Stop N Shop made an offer on the land. That reminds me. Would you do me a favor?"

"Sure." I'd reached for the form, but didn't pull it toward me. Something was knocking at the back of my brain, trying to get through, something that said "pay attention."

"Well, Dottie sent me the income tax forms for the partnership. We get them every year, Simon took care of all that, but I have an accountant now, anyway, I can't send that form in. I don't own those shares anymore. I get something, but Mr. Cameron needs this one. I called Dottie and asked her for Mr. Cameron's address, or perhaps his phone number, but she didn't know it. She said Sharon had all the information and— Are you all right, dear?"

I knew I was staring at her with my mouth open. I shut it quickly. "I'm fine. Did Dottie say anything else?"

"Only that Sharon had taken over all the book work for the partnership, and Dottie didn't have anything to do with it anymore. She thought that was strange, so did Hank Sawyer, but Sharon was in charge. She's so efficient. I still don't know what to do with that form. Will you take it back to Sharon, dear?"

There was the link. I knew it, and I knew what it meant, but I didn't believe it. I couldn't. I had to get away and think.

"It's so sweet of you, dear. I hope it's no trouble," Alice prattled on. "But then, you and Sharon do work in the same office. She'd turned out to be such a lovely girl, and she was such a wild child, so messy and willful. After she ran off with that man to Seattle, well, it almost broke her father's heart, but then she came back, right before he died. She's turned out to be quite smart, and so neat! I've never seen anyone dress so well, and so meticulously. I do think that's important, don't you, dear…"

I could hear Alice, but I wasn't listening. I was concentrating on what she had just said. Clothes. The last puzzle piece slid quietly into place, and I could no longer doubt. The horror of what I was thinking must have been expressed on my face, for Alice broke off to say, "Are you feeling well, dear? Perhaps a glass of water…"

She started to get up, but I hurriedly told her, "No, please. I'm fine."

I stuffed everything in my briefcase, snapped it shut and pushed back my chair. I had to get out of there, go home, think this through and call Dan.

"Wait, dear." Alice pushed back her own chair. "I have that tax thing right here—somewhere—I put it…" She rummaged through the top drawer of an old hutch, opened the cupboard door below, pulled out a handful of papers, selected one and gave it to me. Schedule K-1 (Form 1120S) Shareholder's Share of Income, Credits, Deductions, Etc. was printed across the top. I had no idea what that form meant to the IRS, but I had a pretty good idea how it related to murder.

It was a while before I could escape. I had to reassure Alice several more times that I would indeed deliver the partnership form to Sharon and tell her Alice needed a revised one, that she didn't need to paint the fence before we put up the For Sale sign, and that, yes, she probably would need a new wardrobe for Florida. I left her trying to decide if it was too soon to start cleaning out the attic and headed slowly through the empty streets for home.

We had it all wrong, I thought as I drove. All of us had it wrong. It wasn't Tom. It wasn't jealousy. It wasn't Ray, worried about his license. It was Stop N Shop, but not Benjamin. Sharon. All the time it was Sharon.

I drove into my driveway in a daze, walked into the kitchen, threw my coat over a chair, my briefcase on the table, and kept on going into the living room where I dropped into my chair. I had to think this through before I called anyone. Before I called Dan.

First, the dress. Last Sunday Sharon had worn a green wool dress on her way to list the Pierponts' house, but she had on a navy blue suit when she arrived at the Pierponts'. Mrs. Pierpont had mentioned her blue shoes, and that's how she was dressed when she arrived at my house. So, she'd left the office in green, arrived at her listing, late, in blue. Why would she change clothes? Because she had blood on the other ones? And, why was she late? She'd left the office around two, but hadn't arrived at the Pierponts' until four. I knew exactly what time the rain had started. I'd been caught in it, and Mrs. Pierpont had said Sharon came in the middle of the downpour. Then, Mr. Marburger'd said Stop N Shop had been working with Sharon for two years. It was about that time Sharon had put together the partnership, but she hadn't mentioned that store to anyone until a few months ago, months after some of the original partners had been bought out. Who were these new partners? Why had Hank wanted their names, and why wouldn't Sharon give Dottie any information about them? Somehow, Sharon was cheating her old friends through that partnership. I didn't understand quite how, but I knew it. Wait! The night Dottie was killed, Sharon saw Tom go into the AM PM. What was she doing on the streets that late at night? Shooting Dottie? It seemed only too possible.

I found I was shaking. All the little pieces fell into place. I didn't have all of them, but enough to know I was right. I had to get to a phone.

The impersonal voice on the other end informed me Dan wasn't in, and she didn't know when he would return. No, she didn't know where he was. Yes, she would have him call me, and, yes, she understood it was important.

Now what? I let my hand rest on the silent phone. Do I wait? Do I call someone else? Aunt Mary? No, I need to talk to Dan first.

Restlessly, I checked my watch, leafed through

the magazines on the coffee table, threw them all down, picked up my book and stared at the cover without seeing it. Automatically, I reached for the remote and clicked on the TV. Our local station was announcing a newsbreak, advising us to stand by, and suddenly there was Dan, surrounded by reporters. I recognized the San Luis Obispo County Court House behind him. It was hard to make out what he was saying through the babble of reporters, but they fell silent as he started to read a statement, and now it was all too clear. They had arrested Tom.

"No," I shouted at the TV. "You've got it all wrong." I watched, helplessly, wondering how soon Dan would start the thirty-minute drive back to Santa Louisa. Should I call the police station again, or wait? Should I call the TV station? I stared at the TV, which had returned to its old movie, trying to decide, when the doorbell rang. Dan already? I whirled around. Impossible, but I rushed to answer it just the same.

"Aren't you going to invite me in, Ellen?" Sharon brushed past me and walked into the living room, paused to survey the bookcases before she turned.

"Aren't you going to close the door, Ellen? It's chilly outside."

Numbly, I obeyed. The whole world seemed to

be moving in slow motion. Sharon's huge shoulder bag sank slowly down on the arm of the sofa; her coat gently unwound itself and floated down to join it. Each footstep back into my living room seemed to take an eternity and my brain registered nothing. This blissful state of shock didn't last long enough, and thoughts began to tumble over themselves. Why was Sharon here? Did she know I suspected her? How could she know? What should I do? Should I tell her about Tom? Yes, that's what I'd do.

"Did you hear about Tom?" I edged my way around the side of the sofa toward the dining room.

"Tom?" She took her hand off her bag and looked at me thoughtfully. "No, what about him?"

"He's been arrested. I saw it on television." I took another step closer to the dining room.

"Arrested. Hum. That makes things a little easier. Poor Tom. He never was too bright, and Nicole is a featherhead. But they've proved quite useful. Where are you going, Ellen? Surely you aren't trying to avoid my company." This last statement came as I took several more steps toward the door.

"Of course not." I was starting to think again. I didn't know what was going on but alarm bells were ringing. I needed to get to the kitchen and, hopefully, to the back door. "But you're right. It's chilly. I'll just go get us some firewood. How about some coffee? Only take me a minute." I turned to make a dash for the door.

"Don't, Ellen. It's really not a good idea. Stay here with me."

I was staring into the barrel of a deadly looking gun held all too securely in Sharon's hand. It looked quite comfortable there.

"I know what to do with this, Ellen, so please don't make a stupid mistake. Come over here and sit down. We need to talk."

I came back slowly and sank down in my large chair, my eyes never leaving the gun. Sharon walked around in front of the sofa and also sat, facing me.

This isn't happening, I thought as I looked at Sharon's familiar, unchanged face. Small smile, friendly, interested, her professional real estate face. No hint of threat in anything but the gun pointed steadily at my midsection.

"Tell me, Ellen. Did you have a good visit with Alice?"

Alice! Who cared? But I replied, trying not to let my voice shake. "Oh yes, my, yes."

"Did you get the listing?" Sharon persisted with horrible normalcy.

"Yes, I did. You were a big help, Sharon. All your work, I really appreciate it." *What are we doing?* I wanted to scream. *This doesn't matter.*

But it didn't seem I had a choice, so I'd go on playing until Sharon was done. Only, I didn't think I was going to like what happened when she finished her little game.

"Was that when you knew, Ellen? At Alice's?" She was done.

"Knew what?" I hoped I sounded innocent. Maybe I could stall for time, time to do what, I didn't know. Time to think of something, to keep Sharon from using that gun.

"Game's over, Ellen." As if I hadn't figured that out. "Alice called the office, looking for you. She forgot to give you the name of her accountant, but she gave it to me. She told me all about giving you the partnership return, and how upset you seemed. How did you figure it out, Ellen? You don't know a thing about real estate."

The gun went up a little, somewhere about the middle of my chest. I could feel my hands and feet getting very cold, and my heart was starting to constrict. I had no idea what to say, so I blurted out the truth.

"I don't understand it. I don't know what's wrong with that partnership, or how you set it up, but something's wrong. You're cheating all the people who trusted your father, and who tried to help you."

She ignored that and went on, her tone holding only curiosity. "But you knew I'd killed Hank and Dottie. How?" She might have been asking directions to the bus stop for all the emotion she showed. What was worse, I found myself following her lead.

"It was the clothes. When I remembered about the clothes, I was positive."

"Clothes?" She looked blank. Unfortunately, not blank enough to lower the gun.

My words came tumbling out, almost as if I had to impress her. "You had on a green dress Sunday when you left for the Pierponts', and it wasn't raining. Mrs. Pierpont said it was pouring when you arrived. That means you got there right at four o'clock. Your appointment was for two o'clock. Then, when you came to my house, you had on a navy blue suit. Somewhere during those two hours, you changed. When I wondered why, there was only one answer. Then, the gun. Tom always parks in the same place, and he never locks his car. You had as much opportunity as Ray or Benjamin, and you couldn't help but know about it. Everyone else did."

"Anything else?" A ghost of a smile passed across Sharon's face.

Like the snake following the flute, I kept my eye on the gun, which never wavered. "Mr. Marburger."

For the first time, Sharon looked startled. "Mr. Marburger! What about him?"

"He told me how long you have been working with Stop N Shop on the purchase of that land. You lied about that."

"You really are clever, Ellen." At any other time I would have taken it as a compliment. "The clothes, the Pierponts, I never thought about that. Luckily, no one else will either. This is such a shame, Ellen, but you do see I have no choice."

She seemed to be raising the gun and panic pierced me like an arrow. Or a bullet. Time. I had to get more time, but how?

"Wait!" I almost shouted, putting up my hand. "Tell me about the partnership." I could feel sweat forming at my temples but didn't dare reach up to wipe it off. "I don't understand that part at all."

"Neither did Hank," Sharon said scornfully. "The fool. He had it backwards, but he'd figured out enough to be dangerous." Her hand relaxed slightly, and the gun descended a fraction. "All right, but listen carefully. I'm only going to tell you once."

Then make it long, I prayed, *long and complicated.*

"Stop N Shop is based in Seattle. I knew they were looking for a site in our area before I came home. I knew that land across the river was perfect for them, and it was cheap. I didn't have enough money to buy it, or even to secure it, so I put together that partnership. Later, when I found out how much Stop N Shop was prepared to pay, I knew I needed a bigger share. A much bigger share." Sharon told the first part calmly, impressed with her own cleverness, but now her eyes narrowed and her voice rose a little. "All those old people who bought in, they already had money, lots of it, and they didn't even care. But I did. I do. That money is my way out of this horrible place. This isn't a sleepy town. It's a prison filled with nasty, small-minded people who have always hated me. They thought I was no good as a girl, and they were jealous when I came back and became successful. I'm getting out, and the sweetest part is they're going to provide the way."

A wildness crept into Sharon's eyes that terrified me even more, something I wouldn't have believed possible. She went on, each sentence coming a little faster, as if she'd stored all this up too long, and was finally getting a chance to vent her bitterness.

"That was when I invented the new partners. I borrowed against everything my father had left me, and started buying the old people out."

"You're Paul Cameron?"

"Of course. Why do you think I couldn't send

out IRS partnership returns? Why do you think I took all the book work away from Dottie? She was already suspicious. She's the one who told Hank, only they both thought I'd brought in ringers, outside people who would make the big profits and ease out the locals. Hank had Dottie snooping around, trying to find— Ellen, are you listening to me?"

"Of course." I tried to keep my face blank. I'd heard the soft purr of an engine in my driveway. Dan? *Oh, please, God, let it be Dan.*

Sharon heard it also. I could see her back stiffen, and the finger on the trigger tightened.

"Who...?" was all she got out before the back door slammed.

"Phone you tonight," a familiar voice called out. "Mom?" The car backed down the driveway, and footsteps sounded in the dining room. Dear God, no. Not Susannah!

"Don't come in here," I screamed.

"Why?" She walked into the room and stopped short. Her mouth opened a little as she stared at Sharon and the gun. "Oh."

Sharon was on her feet, smiling at Susannah, motioning her into the room. "This must be your daughter. Come sit beside your mother, that's right. Right there."

Susannah advanced slowly, transferring her

stare from the gun to me. "What...?" was all she managed to say.

"This is Sharon Harper." The unreality of this ridiculous introduction almost made me laugh. Or have hysterics. "She seems to want to—ah—to—ah..." I couldn't bring myself to say out loud that Sharon was going to shoot me, and now Susannah as well.

Sharon wasn't having the same difficulty. "Such a pretty girl. Too bad you came home when you did, for I'm sure you understand I can't leave you alive either, not now."

"Of course I don't understand." Reality had not quite taken hold yet. "What's going on here? Why do you want to shoot my mother? Or me?"

Keep talking, baby, I thought, for suddenly I had an idea. Jake had appeared from behind the set of Dickens, stretched and started his pre-dinner bath. He looked curiously down at our little scene.

"It seems Sharon killed Hank and Dottie." I tried to keep my eyes off the shelf.

"Why? What's that got to do with killing us?" Susannah was starting to believe this was real and alarm was building.

"Never mind," Sharon snapped at her. Tension was building in her as well. I was running out of time. The gun was rising again.

"But..." Susannah protested.

I took a deep breath and whistled. Sharon jerked, startled. Susannah threw herself to the side and yelled, "Duck!"

That was the last thing I wanted to do, as Jake sailed down from the bookcase, right on cue, landing on the back of the sofa first, then with one more leap, in my arms. Sharon screamed, but didn't let go of the gun. I screamed also, to Susannah to get out of there, and heaved poor Jake right in Sharon's face. Susannah flung herself forward, towards Sharon, Jake and the gun. She'd get shot for sure. "No. Don't," I yelled, and jumped after her. Now we were all screaming and clawing at each other. I had a sleeve, and dropped it as a foot hit my mouth. Somewhere, I heard a crash. A lamp? A chair? I neither knew nor cared. I had to find that gun. Susannah was in the middle of thrashing bodies, and all I could think of was how to keep her from getting shot! Someone's thumb was in my eye, someone's teeth dug into my arm, Jake's I thought, and I had a handful of hair, whose, I didn't know. Then the gun went off. The explosion was fierce. I heard a thud, followed by the tinkle of broken glass and a faint meow. Someone human groaned. Hands were on me, lifting me, pulling me. I swung wildly and hit only air.

"Quit fighting, Ellie. The cavalry's arrived."

The voice was most welcome. Through my tears and straggly hair I saw Dan's face.

I found myself leaning against him. He didn't seem to mind. Gary and a policewoman I'd never seen before were struggling with Sharon, trying to snap on handcuffs, much too gently I thought. She was not submitting silently. Gary's face turned red as he listened.

"Extensive vocabulary," Dan commented, his arm tight around me. "I never would have guessed. Wonder if she'll shut up long enough for us to read her her rights?"

I looked around at my savaged living room. Lamp on the floor, table overturned, broken glass on the carpet, Susannah slumped against the wall. Oh, my God, Susannah. She sat, legs out, head down, hair streaming over her face. *She's dead,* I thought, *my beautiful daughter, and it's my fault.* I tore myself away from Dan and hurtled across the room, calling her name. I knelt before her, reached out to smooth the hair from her eyes, tears streaming from my own. Relief flooded through me when she stirred and lifted her head. She pushed herself higher against the wall, surveyed the scene being played out in the room, then looked up at me. "Tell me, Mom. Is it going to be this much fun every time I come home?"

TWENTY-NINE

IT HAD BEEN several hours since Gary and the policewoman had dragged Sharon out of my living room, still kicking, still screaming words I didn't think were in my dictionary. Dan had followed almost immediately, but promised to return as soon as he could.

"I've got a lot of questions for you, Ellie."

"You've got questions? I'm the one who almost got killed."

Aunt Mary had arrived almost before Dan was out the driveway.

"Are you all right?" She examined first me, then Susannah. "I heard one of you got shot. You don't look shot," she said almost accusingly.

"We're fine," I said wearily.

Susannah was more direct. "How did you hear so fast? They only just pulled that Sharon woman out of here."

Aunt Mary was saved from answering by the ring of the doorbell. This time it was Pat, Carl and Neil.

"How did you...?" Poor Susannah. She had yet

to realize email is no substitute for a small-town grapevine.

Coffee was made, a plate of cookies I'd forgotten I had was passed and everyone settled down in my living room, expecting to hear our story.

I started, telling them everything up to when Susannah arrived home. She took over, describing the fight, the gun and the part Jake played, in lurid detail.

"Where is he?" Aunt Mary looked around for the cat.

"Probably under the bed, nursing his dignity back to health." Carl was the vet. He ought to know. But I hoped Jake would come out soon. I owed him an apology. Also a big dinner.

The phone rang. And rang. The press, the TV station, friends, even Susannah's third cousin once removed, they all called, and they all wanted to know everything. Even Susannah finally tired of telling about the gun and the cat.

Finally the living room was empty and the phone silent.

"Do you want anything?" I sat slumped deep in my chair, Jake asleep on my lap. He had evidently forgiven me. I apologized by rubbing his ears.

"Only your boyfriend, Dan, with a full explanation." That's when the doorbell rang.

Stress lines showed deeply around his eyes, but he smiled at both of us, hung his jacket on a peg in the entry, put his arm around me and pulled me close while he delivered a long, very unbrotherly kiss. When he finally let me up for air, he grinned at Susannah.

"Hi, I'm Dan Dunham."

"I'd figured that out."

"I like your Mom."

"So do I." She studied him carefully, then she nodded. "Okay, someone needs to keep an eye on her while I'm gone."

We walked back into the living room, my hand still in Dan's. He stopped, looked at the plates that had held the pizza we'd had delivered, the empty cups and glasses, the crumpled napkins I hadn't yet had the energy to remove and said wistfully, "I don't suppose you have anything left."

"We saved some, and the coffee's fresh and hot," Susannah told him, "but if you tell my mom one thing while I'm not here…"

"I won't." He dropped on the sofa, dragging me down beside him. "Like mother, like daughter," he muttered, as Susannah rushed out toward the kitchen.

He'd finished two pieces and downed a cup of coffee before we got one word out of him.

"Where's Sharon now?" was the first thing Susannah wanted to know. "She's not out on bail, or anything?" There was touch of apprehension in her voice, a feeling I shared.

"Murder One doesn't come with bail. Don't worry. She won't be out anytime soon. She can't seem to stop talking. Her attorney is having apoplexy." Dan grinned a little, but immediately turned serious. "She's completely cracked up. I think she needs a doctor a lot more than that attorney."

"If she's talking that much, you must know everything," I said. "Go back to the beginning, and explain all this."

"Evidently it all happened in stages." He settled himself a little more comfortably on the sofa. The cushion moved, and I slid closer to him. I didn't move away. "Sharon met Mr. Marburger and the Stop N Shop people while she was living in Seattle. When her father got sick, she left the man she'd been living with, who is a developer, and came back home. Sharon's had her brokers' license for years, so it was easy for her to take over the business. She found that piece of land, and realized right away it was exactly the size and location Stop N Shop liked to build on. She didn't have any money, so she put together the partnership, incorporated it, and declared herself president and general manager. Then she started negotiating with Stop N Shop."

"Only she didn't tell any of her partners?" Susannah asked. She was sitting forward, listening to all this intently.

"Not for quite some time." Dan settled himself a little deeper in the cushion. I slid a little closer. He smiled before he went on. "Not until she was positive the deal was going to fly. Now here's where the bad part starts."

I couldn't help it. I stiffened, thinking of Hank and Dottie, their families, all the pain Sharon had caused.

"I don't have to go on." Somehow Dan's arm had slid around me and he squeezed me softly.

"Oh, yes, you do," Susannah told him. "Mom's feeling bad for everybody, I can tell by her face, but she wants to know how all this happened as much as I do."

"That right?" Dan looked down at me.

I looked up at him, gave into temptation, pushed the lock of hair back off his forehead, and nodded emphatically. "Go on."

The look I got before he started again was very nice. "Where was I? Oh, yes. Sharon had negotiated a much higher sales price than even she'd expected, and greed set in. By this time her dad had died, and she borrowed against everything she could to raise cash, and started buying out her partners."

"I understand all that. Where do Hank and Dottie come in?"

"Dottie had always done all the paperwork for the partnership," Dan said, "and when these supposed new partners appeared, she wanted information about them for her files. Sharon, of course, couldn't provide any. They were nothing but names she'd made up, names she didn't want to appear anywhere in any official records."

"Which is why Dottie couldn't give Alice Ives an address for Paul Cameron."

"Right." Dan looked down at me approvingly. He moved his arm a little so I could nestle against him, just a tiny bit. "Sharon managed to keep Dottie from being suspicious until it was time to mail out the Schedule K-1's. Each shareholder has to get one and send it in with their income tax return. Dottie wanted addresses, tax ID numbers, all that. Sharon wasn't about to make that up, so she took over all the book work. At first, Dottie was hurt. Then she told Hank about it, and he got suspicious. Sharon thinks, and I'm sure she's right, Hank put Dottie up to getting him the new names."

"Sharon told me Hank thought she was bringing in outside people to buy out the locals, and make the big profit."

"He probably did," Dan replied. "No one knew a thing about Stop N Shop until after Sharon had used up all her money, and couldn't buy out any more people."

All of a sudden I remembered something. "Tom! I saw on the news you'd arrested Tom. You don't still have him in jail!"

"We never arrest more than one person at a time for any one murder." Dan smiled down at me. A nice kind of a smile. "He's probably home by now, recovering."

"Serves him right," Susannah said heartlessly. "Maybe he'll learn to control his temper."

I started to ask how she knew about Tom's temper problems, but stopped. Maybe she'd learned how to tap into the small-town hotline, but, as long as Tom was free, I really didn't care.

"Was that Tom's gun?" Susannah evidently referred to the one Sharon had tried to use on us.

"It was. Tom has a permit, and it matches."

"So, all the loose ends are tied, except for one. Or maybe two."

"What's that?" asked Dan, surprised. "I thought I told you everything.

"I saw you on television, announcing Tom's arrest, just minutes before Sharon arrived. You were in San Luis Obispo. How did you get back so fast?"

Dan looked blank, then laughed. "I made that

statement early this morning. They ran that thing every half hour all day. I'd been back since noon."

"Okay. Now explain how you knew to turn up here." Susannah held up her hand, and hastily said, "Not that I'm complaining."

"Actually," Dan said a little slowly, carefully not looking at me, "we've been a little interested in that partnership ourselves. I think Sharon knew that, because she'd taken all of the files home. She evidently spent all day Friday holed up, going through them, throwing out anything that might incriminate her."

That explained why I got stuck with Mr. Marburger, but I didn't stop to think about that. "You didn't tell me!" I sat straight up. "I could have been killed! So could Susannah!"

"No, I didn't tell you," Dan admitted. "It seemed the right thing at the time. I'd no idea all these people, Mr. Marburger, Alice Ives, Mrs. Pierpont, had pieces of the puzzle, and that they'd pass them on to you. We were working from a completely different end."

"You still didn't say how you knew we needed you," Susannah insisted.

"We were looking for Sharon. More and more, it was evident she was deeply involved in something. If not in murder, certainly in fraud. One of my officers saw her car in front of your house and called in. It seemed a perfect time for a little interference."

"Just like in the movies, or one of Mom's books," Susannah said. "Boy, were we glad to see you."

"Always nice to be wanted." Dan grinned at Susannah, then smiled much differently down on me.

"Will you look who's back." There was Jake, standing at Dan's end of the sofa, tail slightly twitching, looking thoughtfully at Dan's lap. He gave me a disdainful look, sailed up on Dan's legs and started to purr. I may have been forgiven for throwing him at Sharon, but not for setting him down when Dan came in. Besides, it seemed Dan gave better ear rubs.

Dan took his arm from around my shoulders and started to scratch Jake's ears. "Had a bad morning, didn't you, old fellow." He crooned to the cat, who crooned back with a loud purr. I looked first at Dan, then meaningfully at the cat.

"We'll have to give some thought on how to work this out, won't we?" Dan laughed.

"Oh, I think we can find a way." Susannah walked across the room, scooped Jake up in her arms and headed for the kitchen. "Come on, you hero you, let's go call Neil." Without a backward glance, she quietly closed the door.

* * * * *

REQUEST YOUR FREE BOOKS!

2 FREE NOVELS
PLUS 2 FREE GIFTS!

WORLDWIDE LIBRARY®
MYSTERY
Your Partner in Crime

YES! Please send me 2 FREE novels from the Worldwide Library® series and my 2 FREE gifts (gifts are worth about $10). After receiving them, if I don't wish to receive any more books, I can return the shipping statement marked "cancel." If I don't cancel, I will receive 4 brand-new novels every month and be billed just $5.24 per book in the U.S. or $6.24 per book in Canada. That's a saving of at least 34% off the cover price. It's quite a bargain! Shipping and handling is just 50¢ per book in the U.S. and 75¢ per book in Canada.* I understand that accepting the 2 free books and gifts places me under no obligation to buy anything. I can always return a shipment and cancel at any time. Even if I never buy another book, the two free books and gifts are mine to keep forever.

414/424 WDN FEJ3

Name	(PLEASE PRINT)

Address		Apt. #

City	State/Prov.	Zip/Postal Code

Signature (if under 18, a parent or guardian must sign)

Mail to the **Reader Service:**
IN U.S.A.: P.O. Box 1867, Buffalo, NY 14240-1867
IN CANADA: P.O. Box 609, Fort Erie, Ontario L2A 5X3

Not valid for current subscribers to the Worldwide Library series.

Want to try two free books from another line?
Call 1-800-873-8635 or visit www.ReaderService.com.

* Terms and prices subject to change without notice. Prices do not include applicable taxes. Sales tax applicable in N.Y. Canadian residents will be charged applicable taxes. Offer not valid in Quebec. This offer is limited to one order per household. All orders subject to credit approval. Credit or debit balances in a customer's account(s) may be offset by any other outstanding balance owed by or to the customer. Please allow 4 to 6 weeks for delivery. Offer available while quantities last.

Your Privacy—The Reader Service is committed to protecting your privacy. Our Privacy Policy is available online at www.ReaderService.com or upon request from the Reader Service.

We make a portion of our mailing list available to reputable third parties that offer products we believe may interest you. If you prefer that we not exchange your name with third parties, or if you wish to clarify or modify your communication preferences, please visit us at www.ReaderService.com/consumerschoice or write to us at Reader Service Preference Service, P.O. Box 9062, Buffalo, NY 14269. Include your complete name and address.

WWLI1B

FAMOUS FAMILIES

YES! Please send me the *Famous Families* collection featuring the Fortunes, the Bravos, the McCabes and the Cavanaughs. This collection will begin with 3 FREE BOOKS and 2 FREE GIFTS in my very first shipment— and more valuable free gifts will follow! My books will arrive in 8 monthly shipments until I have the entire 51-book *Famous Families* collection. I will receive 2-3 free books in each shipment and I will pay just $4.49 U.S./$5.39 CDN for each of the other 4 books in each shipment, plus $2.99 for shipping and handling.* If I decide to keep the entire collection, I'll only have paid for 32 books because 19 books are free. I understand that accepting the 3 free books and gifts places me under no obligation to buy anything. I can always return a shipment and cancel at any time. My free books and gifts are mine to keep no matter what I decide.

268 HCN 0387   468 HCN 0387

Name _____ (PLEASE PRINT) _____

Address _____ Apt. # _____

City _____ State/Prov. _____ Zip/Postal Code _____

Signature (if under 18, a parent or guardian must sign) _____

Mail to the **Reader Service:**
IN U.S.A.: P.O. Box 1867, Buffalo, NY 14240-1867
IN CANADA: P.O. Box 609, Fort Erie, Ontario L2A 5X3

ReaderService.com

Manage your account online!

- Review your order history
- Manage your payments
- Update your address

*We've designed
the Reader Service website
just for you.*

Enjoy all the features!

- Reader excerpts from any series
- Respond to mailings and
  special monthly offers
- Discover new series available to you
- Browse the Bonus Bucks catalogue
- Share your feedback

Visit us at:
ReaderService.com

RS12